Acting Edition

I0687891

A Rise in the Market

A Comedy

by Edward Taylor

SAMUEL FRENCH

FOR PRODUCTION INQUIRIES

UNITED STATES AND CANADA
info@concordtheatricals.com
1-866-979-0447

UNITED KINGDOM AND EUROPE
licensing@concordtheatricals.co.uk
020-7054-7298

Each title is subject to availability from Concord Theatricals Corp., depending upon country of performance. Please be aware that *A RISE IN THE MARKET* may not be licensed by Concord Theatricals Corp. in your territory. Professional and amateur producers should contact the nearest Concord Theatricals Corp. office or licensing partner to verify availability.

This work is published by Samuel French, an imprint of Concord Theatricals Corp.

CHARACTERS:

SIR CLIVE PARTRIDGE:
    A senior member of the British Common Market Commission

LADY GILLIAN PARTRIDGE:
    His wife

SIMON PROUT:
    An executive with the British Embassy in Paris

ERNEST KIBBLE:
    A senior clerk at the Embassy

ASTRID:
    A translator with the Common Market Commission in Brussels

LOUISE MULLER:
    An expatriate American, married to a French businessman

JACQUES BERRI:
    President of the Common Market Commission. A Belgian

The action of the play takes place in a luxurious penthouse flat in Paris.

ACT I

(The curtain rises on the elegant lounge area of a penthouse flat in Paris. It is early on a spring evening.)

(On stage-right, an archway leads to the entrance hall and front door. The rear wall has two bedroom doors. The rear stage-left corner is angled to give a balcony, with full-length glass sliding doors. The stage-right corner is angled to provide a small recess, where a door leads into the bathroom. The stage-left wall has a door to the dining-room, and an arched passageway to the kitchen.)

(Voices are heard in the hall. They are those of PROUT and PARTRIDGE, who now enter the lounge. Both are smartly but soberly suited, as befits government executives working abroad: but SIR CLIVE PARTRIDGE's suit is the more expensive, and so is the man inside. At the moment, though, he's in a bad temper.)

PARTRIDGE. How can they lose a blasted suitcase between Bonn and Paris?

PROUT. The Germans are usually so efficient.

PARTRIDGE. Efficient? Hah! The Germans I know couldn't organize a booze-up in a beer-hall!

PROUT. This is the lounge, sir.

PARTRIDGE. Anyway, it was a French plane, so I imagine it's their fault. Scruffy bunch – all they care about is tips. Chap expected one for wheeling an empty trolley – said it wasn't his fault my suitcase was lost. Bloody French are as bad as the blasted Belgians!

PROUT. You were in Bonn for the Assembly?

PARTRIDGE. Yes, I was main speaker on International Friendship. So this is where you're putting me up?

PROUT. I hope you'll be comfortable. As you know, the Embassy has a regular flat for VIP visitors, but that's being repaired and redecorated.

PARTRIDGE. Repaired?

PROUT. Yes, we had a British musical group there last month – they were star guests at the Paris Festival. I'm afraid they caused some damage.

PARTRIDGE. One of these damn pop groups, I suppose.

PROUT. No, it was the Windermere String Quartet. They'd hoped to get the Bach award, but at least they got the Mozart.

PARTRIDGE. Sounds as though they got Brahms and Liszt.

PROUT. I had to find this place in a hurry. But I think it has everything you need.

PARTRIDGE. Drinks?

PROUT. Yes, I've had the cabinet stocked up.

PARTRIDGE. Well, pour me a large Scotch.

PROUT. Of course, sir. *(Under subsequent dialogue, PROUT goes to the drinks cabinet and obliges. PARTRIDGE takes a look round the lounge before sitting down.)* And there's plenty of food in the kitchen. We've taken the place as a going concern. The owner had to go abroad suddenly, on business. Soda, sir? Or water?

PARTRIDGE. Don't be facetious, man.

(PROUT crosses to him with the neat whisky.)

PROUT. Bit of luck, actually. Well, partly luck and partly me moving rather swiftly. Accommodation's always difficult in Paris – but with tomorrow's conference, it's frankly impossible.

PARTRIDGE. Place filling up with foreigners, I suppose.

PROUT. I happened to meet this chap in the United Nations Club at the weekend. French businessman – sudden problem with one of his foreign companies – had to dash off in a hurry.

PARTRIDGE. Aren't you drinking?

PROUT. Thank you no, sir. I don't. Well, very rarely. Sometimes a port at Christmas – for the Queen's speech, you know.

PARTRIDGE. Well, pour yourself a Scotch and I'll drink it for you. In face, you can use my glass.

PROUT. Oh ... er ... thank you. *(PROUT takes PARTRIDGE's empty glass, and refills it.)* Anyway, he wanted to let his flat, furnished, so I grabbed it. Gave him a British Embassy cheque for three months in advance, and got the keys. Oh, I'll let you have them now, while I think of it. I had a copy made, as I gather Lady Partridge is joining you.

PARTRIDGE. Yes, she's coming from Rome.

(PROUT hands a pair of keys to PARTRIDGE.)

PROUT. I'm required to keep one key for the Embassy. I believe you're off on Saturday, sir.

PARTRIDGE. Yes – working-party in Luxembourg. A hundred delegates will be flying in from all parts of Europe.

PROUT. What is the subject?

PARTRIDGE. Congestion of Common Market airspace. But look here – what is the British Embassy doing about my suitcase?

PROUT. They're ringing the airline every hour. And our Mr. Kibble is buying you new socks and underwear. He should be here with them shortly.

PARTRIDGE. I could have done without personal problems. This conference is very important.

PROUT. Indeed, sir, and everyone's rooting for you in tomorrow's election. We all want to see a British President of the Commerce Commission. And you'll be proposed by the retiring President?

PARTRIDGE. So I understand. Monsieur Berri is a puritan – places great value on morality and temperance. Pour me another Scotch, will you?

PROUT. Of course, sir. *(PROUT takes PARTRIDGE's glass and complies.)* It's a tradition that the Conference always elects the President's nominee.

PARTRIDGE. Certainly. He's been impressed by my work for the Purity League.

PROUT. So are we all, sir.

PARTRIDGE. I was active in keeping obscene films out of Britain, you know. Had to sit through hundreds of 'em. Some several times.

PROUT. And you've also distinguished yourself in European matters. I believe you proposed the rules about Common Market eggs?

PARTRIDGE. Certainly. They're required to come in five different grades, at not less than a billion eggs a week.

PROUT. Is that legally binding?

PARTRIDGE. Absolutely.

PROUT. And aren't you sorting out the Milk Mountain?

PARTRIDGE. I have already done so.

PROUT. What exactly was the problem there?

PARTRIDGE. Lot of damn nonsense. The French hill-farmers had trouble with their milk-yield – the cows don't like being milked on the slant. They marched into Paris.

PROUT. The cows?

PARTRIDGE. The farmers. We trebled the milk subsidy so they could make a fat living out of not much milk. Then all the farmers in Europe started breeding more cows to get the subsidy – greedy devils. We thought of getting them sterilized.

PROUT. The farmers?

PARTRIDGE. The cows. We finished up with a huge milk surplus. Monsieur Berri dumped it in my lap last week.

PROUT. Nasty.

PARTRIDGE. I've found the answer – we're selling it cheap to the Russians. The stuff started moving yesterday, in a fleet of refrigerated lorries.

PROUT. Monsieur Berri must be pleased.

PARTRIDGE. He will be. He's calling here tonight to hear the outcome.

PROUT. Monsieur Berri's coming here?

PARTRIDGE. And it seems I'll be greeting him in the clothes I travelled in.

PROUT. I'm sure my colleague will be here soon with some fresh things. Perhaps you'd like to see round the flat, Sir Clive? *(PROUT starts moving around, opening doors and indicating things: apparently under the impression that PARTRIDGE is following. But PARTRIDGE remains sitting heavily in his chair.)* You have two bedrooms ... both with beds, of course ... I think you'll find this balcony rather pleasant ... self-locking door, for security ... *(PROUT turns the catch, and slides the balcony door open.)* Shall I leave it open? It's rather a pleasant evening ... from here you can see the Embassy, just over the road ... I hope you'll regard that as a convenience ...

PARTRIDGE. It's certainly built like one.

PROUT. This door leads to the dining-room ... ah, and you have a useful device here ... *(PROUT opens a small, safe-like, door: halfway up the stage-left wall.)* My businessman friend has a shredder, to destroy any sensitive papers – precaution against industrial espionage. Put confidential waste in here and it's automatically shredded on its way to the rubbish incinerator in the basement ...

(PROUT closes the shredder door.)

PARTRIDGE. *(Standing up.)* I'm going to have a bath.

PROUT. *(Continuing)* ... the kitchen is through there ...

PARTRIDGE. I have to bath in the kitchen?

PROUT. No, no, of course not, Sir Clive. The bathroom is over here ... allow me to start running it for you ... I expect you'll want to undress ...

PARTRIDGE. That is my habit, yes. Bedroom through here, you say.

(PARTRIDGE goes into the stage-right bedroom, nearest the bathroom, leaving the door half-open. PROUT enters the bathroom, continuing his commentary.)

PROUT. The Ambassador felt I'd done rather well to find this place in a hurry. The great thing with a lived-in flat is, you can be sure everything's working smoothly.

(PROUT has turned on the bathroom taps, and we hear simultaneously a hostile hissing and spurting from them, and a fierce rumbling and banging from the kitchen boiler.)

PARTRIDGE. *(From the bedroom.)* Good God, what's that? World War Three?

PROUT. *(Shouting from bathroom.)* Seems to be a little trouble with the boiler, sir. Probably an air-lock. *(Both noises stop: PROUT has turned the taps off. From bathroom:)* Give it a moment to disperse. Hasn't been used for a day or two. This Continental plumbing sometimes works better if you surprise it. Now then. *(Both noises start again: PROUT has turned the taps on. The kitchen boiler is thundering alarmingly. Then the noises stop, as PROUT turns the taps off. PROUT emerges from the bathroom, en route for the kitchen.)* It shouldn't be doing that, sir. I think I'd better have a look at the heater.

(As PROUT reaches the kitchen, the front-door bell rings.)

PARTRIDGE. *(Calling from bedroom.)* Is that the front-door? My wife's not due yet.

PROUT. It's all right, Sir Clive, it's probably my colleague from the Embassy.

PARTRIDGE. Well, you deal with it – I'd like a bit of privacy.

(The bedroom door is closed from within by PARTRIDGE. PROUT crosses and goes out to the hall. We hear him opening the front door, and talking to the visitor, who speaks English with a slight Belgian accent. This is ASTRID, an attractive intelligent girl in her early twenties. She is in determined mood.)

PROUT. Oh ... Lady Partridge? Do come in – we weren't expecting you yet.

ASTRID. Sir Clive is here?

PROUT. Yes, he arrived a few minutes ago. I'm from the British Embassy, Simon Prout ... *(By now, PROUT and ASTRID have entered the lounge.)* I'll tell Sir Clive you're here, Lady Partridge.

ASTRID. Please do. But I am not Lady Partridge.

PROUT. I'm sure he'll be ... you're not? Oh well, I'm sorry, I don't think Sir Clive will be able to see you. He can't see anyone this evening.

ASTRID. Then tell him to put his glasses on. He'll certainly want to see me.

PROUT. I don't think you quite understand ...

(As PROUT starts to speak. PARTRIDGE opens the bedroom door and comes out, wearing an exotic kimono – having removed his suit, which he is carrying on a hanger, together with his shirt.)

PARTRIDGE. I must say, your friend's got a funny taste in dressing-gowns. I feel like Suzie Wong. Any chance of getting this suit quick-cleaned, d'you think ... *(As he sees ASTRID, PARTRIDGE's jaw drops. He appears stunned, and suit and shirt fall to the floor.)* Good God, what are you doing here?

ASTRID. We have to have a talk.

PARTRIDGE. Talk? Now? We can't ... I mean ... look ...

(As PARTRIDGE boggles, the boiler starts to rumble ominously again. Alarmed, PROUT moves off to investigate, stumbling over PARTRIDGE's clothes as he does so. PROUT picks up suit and shirt and puts them on a chair.)

PROUT. Er ... I'd better go and sort out that boiler, sir. Can't think what's the matter. Monsieur Muller didn't say he had trouble with his pipes ...

(PROUT hurries into the kitchen, closing the door behind him. During the next few minutes, there are intermittent rumbles from the boiler, with periods of silence in between.)

PARTRIDGE. For God's sake, Astrid, you're not supposed to be in Paris, you're supposed to be in Brussels! My wife will be here any minute!

ASTRID. All right, who is she?

PARTRIDGE. My wife? She's the woman I'm married to ... vague person, writes poetry ... you know who my wife is!

ASTRID. Not your wife – the woman you have been seeing! All over Europe! At the opera ... the races! Friends have been telling me "Your Clive has a new woman ... young, beautiful" ... who is she? Not your wife – her I can live with.

PARTRIDGE. That's more than I can ... I mean, of course you can't live with her! ... you mustn't even meet her! What's the matter with you? You've always been happy with our scheme.

ASTRID. Now I find out you are more scheming than I thought! The flat in Brussels – all right! The good times together when you are there – all right! The rest of the time you are with your wife who does not understand you, no boom-boom and straight off to sleep – all right!

PARTRIDGE. Keep your voice down, for heaven's sake!

ASTRID. But a third woman, who you take out and flirt with, that is not all right! That is all wrong!

PARTRIDGE. I don't know what you're talking about! I may have attended the odd social function with my secretary ...

ASTRID. Not your secretary – her with the flat shoes and canvas knickers! Everyone has seen you with a glamorous woman!

PARTRIDGE. Nonsense, I don't know any glamorous women – except for you, of course.

ASTRID. You think it is just a game, our affaire! You think it does not matter! For me, it is serious!

PARTRIDGE. If my wife finds out, for me it'll be worse than serious. It'll be tragic!

ASTRID. I will show you how serious it is for me ...

PARTRIDGE. In fact, if *anyone* finds out! You know I'm up for President tomorrow. A hint of scandal and my chance is gone!

(ASTRID has produced a small bottle of tablets from her pocket.)

ASTRID. Two of these tablets will kill me in five minutes! Always I have then ready, in case you desert me!

PARTRIDGE. This chap Berri's a puritan of ... what!? Have you taken leave of your senses, girl? Give those to me!

(PARTRIDGE closes with ASTRID, to try and grab the tablets, but she holds them away from him, at the same time striving to unscrew the cap.)

ASTRID. The time has come! Now I will take them! You let me down! I cannot trust you!

(The boiler is quiet and PROUT emerges from the kitchen looking pleased with himself. But his smile disappears as he discovers PARTRIDGE and ASTRID struggling, and hears the last few words. He rushes to assist.)

PROUT. What's happening? Are you all right, sir? I thought you knew this person! I'll call the police!

(PARTRIDGE has succeeded in wrestling the tablets from ASTRID: and the two are now separated, facing each other like wrestlers, panting from the struggle.)

PARTRIDGE. No! No ... it's all right, Prout ... everything's under control ... *(To ASTRID.)* Look, my dear ... calm down ... I'll co-operate. Let's talk this over rationally.

PROUT. But who is this lady? And what are those tablets?

PARTRIDGE. Ah ... er ... who is she? Tablets? You know her, Prout, this is ... er ... tablets, yes ... this is my doctor. Yes. And she's rather cross with me, because I haven't been taking my tablets.

PROUT. Oh, I see. I didn't know you took tablets, sir. Something wrong?

PARTRIDGE. No, nothing ... yes, of course something's wrong. My back. Pain. A martyr to it. Sometimes my life's unbearable. But this lady helps me with ... er ... relieving exercises.

(During the above, PARTRIDGE has located a likely part of his back, and is now holding it ruefully.)

PROUT. A bad back, I am sorry. You must have been doing too much. Work, I mean. How will you manage at tomorrow's conference? Shall I order a wheelchair?

PARTRIDGE. Thank you, Prout, that won't be necessary. My doctor will look after me – won't you, darl ... doctor. You'll see I don't miss the Presidency. As President, I shall spend more time in Brussels.

(ASTRID is weighing up his blandishments, as the boiler resumes its rumbling.)

PROUT. Oh Lord, there it goes again. Excuse me, sir. I hope this doesn't mean you'll be short of hot water ...

(PROUT hurries into the kitchen once more. PARTRIDGE puts the tablets on a table and adopts a conciliatory tone to ASTRID.)

PARTRIDGE. My dear Astrid, you mustn't kill yourself! It could be fatal! This must be all a misunderstanding. There's no other woman in my life.

ASTRID. You swear it? There's no other woman in your life?

PARTRIDGE. I suppose my wife's a sort of woman. But we agreed she didn't count.

ASTRID. You were seen escorting a girl with red hair! At the opera ... at the races ...

PARTRIDGE. Red hair? On her head?

ASTRID. Also in other places!

PARTRIDGE. Other places?

ASTRID. Nightclubs ... restaurants ... you were seen everywhere!

PARTRIDGE. I don't recall escorting a red-haired woman. It must have been coincidence ... someone who happened to be in the same place ...

ASTRID. I can quote dates!

PARTRIDGE. Look, let's not wash our dirty linen in front of our friend from the Embassy, my dear. Let's talk this over in the other room.

ASTRID. Very well, I will give you a little time to explain yourself. But not a lot of time!

PARTRIDGE. Too damn right! My wife will be here in an hour! *(During the above, PARTRIDGE ushers ASTRID towards the bedroom, and follows her in. He pauses at the door and calls to PROUT.)* Prout, my doctor is giving me an examination in the bedroom – we're not to be disturbed.

(PROUT calls back from the kitchen where he has temporarily pacified the boiler, and feels he has diagnosed the problem.)

PROUT. Very good, sir. I think I know your trouble. Your input's too active and your stopcock's too slack. *(PARTRIDGE disappears into the bedroom and closes the door. PROUT emerges from the kitchen, wiping his hands – having, he hopes, completed his plumbing. As he does so, the front-door bell rings, and he goes out to the hall and opens the door. He is heard talking to the new arrival, ERNEST KIBBLE, an elderly member of the embassy staff, who is somewhat vague.)* Ah, Kibble, you got the clothes.

KIBBLE. I hope these things are suitable – it was rather short notice.

PROUT. Sir Clive will be grateful for anything. I'll let him have them at once.

KIBBLE. Er ... might I come in, Mr. Prout? I have some rather alarming news.

PROUT. Can't it wait?

KIBBLE. I think not, Mr. Prout, it's extremely urgent.

PROUT. Oh, very well.

KIBBLE. Thank you, Mr. Prout.

(During ensuing dialogue, PROUT and KIBBLE enter the lounge. KIBBLE is carrying a large brown-paper parcel, which he forgets to put down – holding it, instead, first under one arm and then the other.)

PROUT. Sir Clive will want this place to himself as soon as possible. He's involved in some delicate discussions.

KIBBLE. Yes, I'm sure.

PROUT. His wife will be here shortly, and then he's entertaining Monsieur Berri.

KIBBLE. The President of the Commerce Commission?

PROUT. That's right. They won't be disturbed here. It's lucky I got this flat from my friend Muller, eh?

KIBBLE. Er ... well, yes and no.

PROUT. What d'you mean, 'yes and no'?

PARTRIDGE. Er ... yes, they will be disturbed ... and no, it isn't lucky you got this flat.

PROUT. What's that supposed to mean?

KIBBLE. The police came to the Embassy, Mr. Prout, asking about Monsieur Muller.

PROUT. Monsieur Muller? My good friend Muller, who owns this flat?

KIBBLE. That's right – Monsieur Max Muller. Only it seems he doesn't own the flat.

PROUT. He doesn't own the flat?

KIBBLE. It belongs to his wife. Monsieur Muller had no right to let it.

PROUT. Good grief! How did they know he *had* let it?

KIBBLE. They didn't. They came to ask if we knew where Monsieur Muller was.

PROUT. Monsieur Muller had to go abroad. He wanted to sort out some business.

KIBBLE. Er, no. He wanted to stay out of jail.

PROUT. Jail?

KIBBLE. It appears he's been involved in some dubious activities. He was facing arrest in a currency case. Now he's disappeared.

PROUT. But ... why did the police come to the Embassy?

KIBBLE. They'd heard he was a friend of yours.

PROUT. Muller's not a friend of mine! I only met him twice!

KIBBLE. We told the police you'd only met him through leasing this flat. And they told us it wasn't his to let.

PROUT. Not his flat?

KIBBLE. Apparently it's owned by his wife – the police mentioned her name ... what was it now? ... oh yes, Madame Muller. A Transatlantic person.

PROUT. You mean, she comes from America?

KIBBLE. That's right. Today.

PROUT. What?

KIBBLE. She comes from America today. She's been there on holiday.

PROUT. She's coming here?!

KIBBLE. I expect so. It's her home, you see. She owns it. That's why I thought I should warn you. There could be some confusion.

PROUT. Confusion? There'll be an execution! The Ambassador will kill me! Sir Clive sharing a flat with a crook's wife? And his own wife? And Monsieur Berri calling? Kibble, this could finish my career! I'm ruined.

KIBBLE. Well, we all have our troubles, Mr. Prout. I've got those twinges in my back again.

PROUT. *(In desperation.)* I don't believe it! I simply don't believe it!

KIBBLE. It's true. Just between the shoulder blades – the bit you can't reach.

PROUT. I don't believe there's a woman living here! There'd have been signs ... clothes, knick-knacks ...

(PROUT charges into the unoccupied stage-left bedroom to look around.)

KIBBLE. It comes right up from the base of the spine. Of course, they don't give you proper shirt-tails these days.

(From the bedroom, we hear sounds of PROUT searching, then opening a wardrobe and getting a nasty shock.)

PROUT. *(Off)* Oh, My God!

KIBBLE. And then the Ambassador won't let us wear cardigans on duty. I could have arthritis for all he cares.

(PROUT emerges from the bedroom, looking crestfallen.)

PROUT. There's a wardrobe full of women's clothes. And a jar of cold cream on the dressing table!

KIBBLE. I'm afraid cold cream does no good at all. For one thing, I can't rub it in.

PROUT. Kibble, what are you drivelling about? I tell you, some wretched woman's going to arrive and embarrass Sir Clive!

KIBBLE. No, surely, *I* told *you* that.

PROUT. Don't quibble, Kibble! What can we do? Muller's wife will be here any minute!

KIBBLE. I mean, that's why I ... oh no, not just yet, Mr. Prout. It seems Mrs. Muller arrives on the eight o'clock plane.

PROUT. Thank God! That gives us time to sort something out! Any ideas?

KIBBLE. I find it quite hard to think at the moment. These back pains in my back, you know.

PROUT. Well, I can help you there. Sir Clive has back-trouble himself – his doctor's given him some pills to ease the pain. I could have a word ... ah no, there they are.

(PROUT has spotted ASTRID's tablet-bottle on the table. He picks it up and unscrews the top.)

KIBBLE. Oh. D'you think they'd do the trick?

PROUT. Worth a try, eh? You may get a surprise!

KIBBLE. Oh well ... what is it they say? Kill or cure! *(KIBBLE at last puts down his brown-paper parcel, to receive the tablets.)* This back trouble ruins my life.

PROUT. With a bit of luck, these'll put an end to it.

KIBBLE. Mind you, I'm not all that keen on pills. One doesn't want to become dependent.

(PROUT is tipping pills into his own hand.)

PROUT. Two should do the trick ... well, perhaps three to make sure.

KIBBLE. *(Cheerful)* D'you know, Mr. Prout, the pain's gone now. I think I got it from carrying that parcel. I shan't need the pills after all.

(PROUT tips the pills back, replaces the cap, and puts down the bottle.)

PROUT. Well, it's up to you, Kibble. They're there if you want them. Look, Sir Clive's only staying here for two days. If we could keep Madame Muller away that long, the problem's solved.

KIBBLE. But how can you do that?

PROUT. D'you know exactly where Max Muller's gone?

KIBBLE. No. I thought you'd know.

PROUT. Well, I don't. Perhaps you can find out through the Embassy. Or the police.

KIBBLE. I'll try, Mr. Prout.

PROUT. Good man. I'll stay here, intercept Madame Muller the minute she arrives, and say her husband wants her to join him at once.

KIBBLE. An excellent idea. It's that kind of thinking that makes you an executive.

PROUT. Thank you.

KIBBLE. What a pity you can't do that.

PROUT. It's just a question of ... what? Why can't I do it?

KIBBLE. You can't stay here, Mr. Prout – the Police Inspector wants you back at the Embassy. To tell him about Mr. Muller.

PROUT. But I can't! Not now! My career's at stake! I'll see him tomorrow! I can't possibly come to the Embassy now!

KIBBLE. Then he'll be over here, asking you questions in front of Sir Clive.

PROUT. I'll come to the Embassy now. We've got two hours – I can spare the police ten minutes. God knows why this had to happen just when everything was running smoothly.

(Suddenly the kitchen boiler produces further alarming rumbles.)

KIBBLE. Apart from losing Sir Clive's luggage.

PROUT. And that infernal boiler! What's it doing now? The taps aren't even running!

KIBBLE. Ah, I've heard that noise before. My Aunt Elsie's boiler made a noise like that. We didn't let it worry us. Uncle George said he'd fix it when his leg was better.

PROUT. And did he?

KIBBLE. No – in the end he didn't need to.

PROUT. It stopped of its own accord?

KIBBLE. In a way, yes. It blew up.

PROUT. Good grief!

KIBBLE. Uncle George said afterwards we should have loosened the valve-tappets.

PROUT. Valve-tappets? D'you know where to find them?

KIBBLE. I think so.

PROUT. Well then, for God's sake, let's do it! Quick!

(PROUT hurries KIBBLE into the kitchen.)

KIBBLE. Of course, this may be a different model. Aunt Elsie lived in Saffron Walden.

(PROUT and KIBBLE are in the kitchen, dealing with the boiler, which will produce diminishing rumbles during the next few

minutes. As they close the kitchen-door behind them, the door of
the stage-right bedroom opens, and PARTRIDGE emerges with a
penitent ASTRID.)

ASTRID. I'm sorry, Poochy ... I am too hasty ... always I jump to
the wrong confusion ...

PARTRIDGE. It's all right, my dear, I understand how you felt.
Besides, I should have remembered sooner about my wife.

ASTRID. What made her dye her hair red?

PARTRIDGE. Who know what makes women do anything? I just
got home and found she had red hair. She kept it red for several weeks.
Then she went back to blonde again.

ASTRID. Does she often change her colour?

PARTRIDGE. Constantly. She dyes her hair at the drop of a hat.
That's why it slipped my mind when you first mentioned it.

ASTRID. And I thought my Poochy was with another woman.

PARTRIDGE. *(Laughing it off.)* And all the time I was with my
wife!

ASTRID. Now Poochy, you know I don't mind your seeing your
wife. I object only with women you might make love to.

PARTRIDGE. Yes, yes, my sweet. Well, I'm glad you don't mind
my seeing my wife – but I don't think we should let my wife see you.
And her plane gets in at seven-thirty. So ...

ASTRID. Oh Poochy, then we have an hour. We could go to bed,
yes?

PARTRIDGE. Er, we couldn't go to bed, no. Er ... the sheets
aren't aired. And you know I hate to rush these things. Besides, there's
this idiot here from the Embassy. We have to be discreet. Tomorrow I
have an election.

ASTRID. Tomorrow is too late. I shall be back in Brussels.

PARTRIDGE. No, no, you must be back in Brussels tonight. If
you go now, you can catch the early plane.

ASTRID. But Poochy, it's been weeks ...

(ASTRID is now affectionate, and slides her hand inside
PARTRIDGE's kimono, to caress his chest. PARTRIDGE is torn
between lust and anxiety as the kitchen door opens, the boiler

having subsided, and PROUT and KIBBLE enter. PROUT is taken aback.)

PROUT. Oh, I'm sorry, Sir Clive. I thought your doctor was seeing you in the bedroom.

PARTRIDGE. Er ... yes, yes. We've done the main examination. She just wanted to feel my chest.

PROUT. I thought the pain was in your back.

PARTRIDGE. Oh certainly, yes, that's where the main pain is ... *(PARTRIDGE puts his hand to his back, clearly trying to recall where he clutched it before.)* ... but it can come through, you know. One has to be careful. It can damage the heart on its way across.

PROUT. Oh. This is my colleague, Mr. Kibble. They're still searching for your luggage, but he's brought you new socks and underwear and things.

(PROUT indicates the brown-paper parcel which KIBBLE put down earlier.)

KIBBLE. I'm sorry I couldn't bring it sooner, Sir Clive. I had to deliver some things to the Embassy Players.

PARTRIDGE. Embassy Players?

PROUT. Our Amateur Operatic Group. We're mounting the Yeomen of the Guard.

PARTRIDGE. Indeed?

PROUT. To coincide with tomorrow's conference. Show the flag, you know. A gala performance in the Palace of Culture. I hope you'll be able to attend.

PARTRIDGE. Ah ... er ... unfortunately not. A prior engagement.

PROUT. It's every night this week.

PARTRIDGE. Several prior engagements. Well, thank you ... er ...

PROUT. Prout, sir.

PARTRIDGE. Quite. I don't think I need detain you fellows any longer. *(Heavily, for ASTRID's benefit.)* My wife will be here shortly. My doctor wants to conclude her check and get away.

KIBBLE. Oh, is the lady a doctor? Perhaps she could spare a moment to look at my back ... I had these twinges earlier ...

(KIBBLE has started to take off his jacket, but PROUT checks him.)

PROUT. Not now, Kibble.

PARTRIDGE. I'm sure we'd all be happy to see your back, Mr. Kibble. But my doctor hasn't time at the moment.

(PROUT is ushering KIBBLE out.)

PROUT. Nor have we, Sir Clive. We're expected back at the Embassy. I shall call again later to, er, check you have everything you want.

PARTRIDGE. No need, no need.

PROUT. Er ... I'm sure the Ambassador will insist. Come along, Kibble. I'll see you later, sir.

(PROUT hustles KIBBLE out into the hall: and in a moment we hear the front door close.)

PARTRIDGE. My dear Astrid, you very nearly got me into a great deal of trouble. And I'm sorry, there just isn't time for games tonight.

ASTRID. All right, Poochy. If you promise to visit me in Brussels very soon.

PARTRIDGE. Very soon, my dear. If I can land this job as President of the Commerce Commission. I'll be there very often. With time on my hands and money to burn.

ASTRID. As President, you will be well paid?

PARTRIDGE. All EEC executives get huge salaries for not much work. Hence the phrase "E.E.C. money."

ASTRID. Well then, I shall go now. And I wish you luck. And I hope you enjoy your stay in this flat. It is pleasant, yes?

PARTRIDGE. Apart from the boiler having a nasty attack of indigestion.

(The tension gone, ASTRID feels she has time to look round the flat, sizing things up in the way women do. She is moving around, looking at the furniture and decor.)

ASTRID. But it is quite elegant, no?

PARTRIDGE. I must say, it's better than I'd expect from that fellow Prout. He looks a fool. Well, he is a fool.

ASTRID. It is bigger than my apartment in Brussels.

PARTRIDGE. My dear Astrid, if I get this job, you can have a flat twice this size. You'll be Official Chandler to the Commerce Commission.

ASTRID. Chandler? What will that entail?

PARTRIDGE. Supplying the President's oats. Now, I think you should get a move on, my dear.

ASTRID. And you have a balcony!

(The front-door bell rings.)

PARTRIDGE. Oh Lord, that idiot Prout's forgotten something! *(As ASTRID wanders out through the open balcony door to inspect the view, PARTRIDGE moves to open the front door. As he does so, a surprise awaits him.)* Yes, what is it ... Gillian!

GILLIAN. Hello, Clive.

PARTRIDGE. My God! ... Good Lord! ... I mean, how lovely to see you!

GILLIAN. Well, can I come in?

PARTRIDGE. Come in? ... Yes, yes of course ... *(He speaks extra loud.)* ... A man doesn't want to keep his wife standing on the doorstep!

(ASTRID hears the message, as intended. After freezing in horror for a moment, she hides behind a tall shrub, which stands in a tub on the balcony. As she does so, PARTRIDGE and his wife are crossing the hall, talking, and now enter the lounge. LADY GILLIAN PARTRIDGE is a rather bemused woman in her thirties or early forties, mildly eccentric, and usually pre-occupied. She carries a small overnight bag.)

GILLIAN. I thought you were sending a car to the airport, Clive.

PARTRIDGE. Yes, yes, everything was laid on. But your plane wasn't due till seven-thirty.

GILLIAN. It's all chaotic. There are some people called air traffic controllers, apparently, and the man said they're working to rule, so all the flights are getting in early.

PARTRIDGE. Er ... yes ... splendid. I expect you'd like to pop in the bedroom and change, or lie down, or something. Jacques Berri is calling later.

GILLIAN. My luggage is still at the airport. There was no-one there from the Embassy to see it through Customs.

PARTRIDGE. Well, at least you know where yours is. My case got lost on the flight from Bonn.

GILLIAN. Oh dear, you are so careless, Clive. *(Looking around.)* And this isn't our normal place in Paris, is it?

PARTRIDGE. No, the Embassy found this in a hurry. Their usual VIP flat was vandalized by the Windermere String Quartet.

GILLIAN. I can't say I care for it much – that wallpaper makes me feel quite dizzy.

PARTRIDGE. Well, it's only for a couple of days, my dear. Now that's the bedroom – I'm sure you've things to do in there ...

(PARTRIDGE is anxious to bundle his wife into the stage-right bedroom, but she shows no inclination to go. She is sizing up the flat.)

GILLIAN. Oh, at least we have a balcony ...

(LADY PARTRIDGE moves across, obviously intending to go out onto the balcony. But PARTRIDGE rushes ahead of her, slides the balcony door shut, and stands with his back against the catch.)

PARTRIDGE. No, no, you don't want to go out there, my dear.

GILLIAN. Whyever not?

PARTRIDGE. It's much too cold. These spring evenings can be very treacherous.

GILLIAN. It seemed quite warm on the way from the airport.

PARTRIDGE. Ah, but we're higher up, you see. The air is thinner. Now I mustn't keep you talking – you'll be tired after the flight – why don't you have a lie-down? This is the second bedroom ...

(PARTRIDGE opens the door of the stage-left bedroom and guides his wife in, shutting the door behind them. It seems an opportunity for ASTRID to make her escape, and she darts out from behind her shrub. She tries to slide open the balcony door, but it won't open from the outside. Frustrated, she looks round for something to gouge it with: but then she senses that the PARTRIDGES are about to come out of the bedroom and hurries back behind the shrub. The PARTRIDGES emerge.)

GILLIAN. Rather poky for a second bedroom, I'd have thought.

PARTRIDGE. Well, they did say it was an emergency, my dear. And the other bedroom is rather larger ...

GILLIAN. I wonder why they didn't just book us into the Hotel Mediterranean, where we spent our honeymoon?

PARTRIDGE. I didn't think we liked the Hotel Mediterranean. You said the central heating was overpowering. Or was it me?

GILLIAN. No, Clive, you weren't overpowering.

(PARTRIDGE has opened the door of the stage-right bedroom, and is ushering his wife in.)

PARTRIDGE. Now this bedroom is quite spacious. And the bed seems very comfortable. Shall I draw the curtains for you?

(Again, having got his wife out of the lounge, PARTRIDGE closes the door behind them. Again, ASTRID springs into action, this time wielding a trowel which she has picked up on the balcony, and tries to lever the glass door open. Again she fails, and ducks back behind the shrub just before the PARTRIDGES re-emerge.)

GILLIAN. I suppose that's a little better – at least there's a table I can write on.

PARTRIDGE. *(Enthusiastically)* Ah, you've some ideas, my dear!

GILLIAN. I had a glimmer as we came over the Pyrennees. I felt the mountain peaks were trying to tell me things.

PARTRIDGE. Then you must go in the bedroom, and get them

down. Strike while the muse is hot. Don't waste time chatting to me. If you want to lock yourself in there for an hour, I won't mind, honestly.

GILLIAN. You know I can't work in a hostile environment. I need to know the place is sympathetic. What's through there?

PARTRIDGE. That's the bathroom. *(Idea)* Of course! You need a bath!

GILLIAN. Pardon?

PARTRIDGE. After the flight! And you said it was awfully hot at the airport! What about a nice relaxing bath?

GILLIAN. In a minute. I've things to do first.

PARTRIDGE. Well, come and look at the bathroom, anyway. It's quite luxurious. There's a bath ... and a wash-basin ... all sorts of things ...

(During the above, PARTRIDGE has been maneuvering his wife into the bathroom. Again he shuts the door behind them. Again ASTRID tries to lever open the balcony door. This time she uses a small gardening fork, hitting the handle with the trowel, to try and force in a prong. As she does so, the boiler rumbles, LADY PARTRIDGE having turned a tap on. Alarmed, LADY PARTRIDGE emerges from the bathroom in a hurry, before ASTRID has time to hide: ASTRID freezes in the middle of the french window.)

GILLIAN. Good God, what's that noise?

PARTRIDGE. *(Following her out.)* Ah, we have a little trouble with the plumbing, my dear. It's continental, you know ...

(PARTRIDGE is horrified to see ASTRID frozen in full view through the french window. He rushes across and stands at the window facing outwards, contorting himself to her pose, so as to hide her from LADY PARTRIDGE.)

GILLIAN. Clive, what on earth are you doing over there?

PARTRIDGE. Er ... we sent for a plumber – I'm looking to see if he's coming.

GILLIAN. Can you see the street from there?

PARTRIDGE. No ... I thought he might come by helicopter ... he's called the Flying Plumber. You'd better turn that tap off, dear, before we have an explosion.

(Baffled by the whole business, LADY PARTRIDGE returns to the bathroom and turns the tap off, which stops the boiler noise. Her absence enables ASTRID to get behind her shrub, and PARTRIDGE to abandon his pose. Quickly he draws the curtains, which are opened and closed by a cord at the side. LADY PARTRIDGE comes out of the bathroom again.)

GILLIAN. This is very tiresome, Clive. And why have you drawn the curtains?

PARTRIDGE. Mustn't let the sunshine spoil other people's furniture.

GILLIAN. But it's twilight now.

PARTRIDGE. These French twilights are very deceptive – the sun might pop out at any moment. Besides, lamplight is so much more romantic.

(Although the translucent curtains let in plenty of light, PARTRIDGE darts across and switches on a standard lamp.)

GILLIAN. This place has a curious aura. Not entirely unsympathetic, and yet I feel an alien presence. I shall go in the bedroom and lie down, before the knot begins to tighten.

PARTRIDGE. Oh absolutely – we don't want you to get knotted. *(Eagerly, PARTRIDGE opens the door of the stage-right bedroom and ushers his wife in.)* Have a good lie-down, Gillian. I must start getting ready for Monsieur Berri. There are supposed to be some clean clothes somewhere. *(LADY PARTRIDGE has wandered into the bedroom when PARTRIDGE, knowing his wife's habits, has a further idea for keeping her out of the way.)* Oh, and I'll get you some of your medicine. *(PARTRIDGE crosses the lounge and picks up a half-full bottle of sherry and a glass from the drinks cabinet. He takes them into the bedroom.)* This'll help you to unwind. That's right, take your shoes off.

(Now reasonably confident that his wife will stay off the scene for a while, PARTRIDGE shuts the bedroom door again, and dashes over to the balcony window. He quickly draws the curtains open, and beckons to ASTRID, who emerges from behind her shrub, still carrying her trowel and fork. Confidently he tries to turn the catch and open the door, but the catch won't budge. There is a ventilator in the French window, through which PARTRIDGE and ASTRID now converse in loud desperate whispers.)

ASTRID. It won't open, Poochy, I kept trying it.
PARTRIDGE. It's not supposed to open from the outside. I have to open from in here.
ASTRID. I've been pushing it with the trowel and everything.
PARTRIDGE. *(Horrified)* Oh God, you've broken the catch!
ASTRID. Well, do something. I can't stay out here all night!
PARTRIDGE. You silly girl ... the tongue's bent ... I need a screwdriver or some sort of lever. *(He tries inserting his little finger, but only succeeds in hurting it.)* Damn and blast! I'll have to find the porter and see if he's got some tools.
ASTRID. Porter?
PARTRIDGE. Concierge ... whatever ... there must be someone downstairs looking after the flats. I'll be as quick as I can – now for God's sake, stay out of sight!

(As PARTRIDGE moves away from the French window, his wife is heard calling from the bedroom.)

GILLIAN. What's going on, Clive? Who are you shouting at?

(PARTRIDGE opens the bedroom door to forestall LADY PARTRIDGE coming out.)

PARTRIDGE. Er ... I was on the phone, my dear ... to the Embassy ... chasing up this lost case. I'm going down to have a word with the porter about it. Shan't be long.

(PARTRIDGE closes the bedroom door, and is about to resume his mission when he notices he's still wearing the kimono. As he

reacts to this, he sees ASTRID signalling to him through the closed window. They resume their whispered conversation through the ventilator.)

ASTRID. Don't go downstairs – there must be some tools in the flat! Try the kitchen!

PARTRIDGE. Worth a look, I suppose. God, this isn't my day, is it!

(PARTRIDGE disappears into the kitchen, closing the door behind him. As he does so, the bedroom door opens and LADY PARTRIDGE emerges. Her sudden appearance catches ASTRID away from her shrub, and the girl darts out of sight to the left, round the protruding corner of the wall. LADY PARTRIDGE has come out thinking her husband is still in the lounge.)

GILLIAN. Have you any aspirins, Clive? This atmosphere gives me a headache. *(Finding the lounge empty, LADY PARTRIDGE assumes SIR CLIVE has gone downstairs.)* Oh well, never mind. *(LADY PARTRIDGE looks round the empty lounge and her eye lights on ASTRID's bottle of tablets.)* Ah! *(She moves across and picks up the bottle, as if about to take some.)* These ought to do something. *(Then she has second thoughts, peers closely at the bottle, and finally puts it down again.)* Perhaps not. They might be those strong ones.

(LADY PARTRIDGE returns to her bedroom, shutting the door behind her. As she does so, PARTRIDGE comes out of the kitchen, carrying a toolbag. He crosses to the balcony door, takes out a screwdriver and starts wrestling with the lock.)

PARTRIDGE. Blasted foreign locks! A good British lock you can open with a credit card! ... Hah! *(PARTRIDGE has succeeded in pushing the tongue back in line, and is able to turn the lock and slide the door open. But ASTRID has vanished. He steps outside and calls her in a loud whisper.)* Astrid? Quick – now's your chance! Astrid? Astrid! Good grief – where's the girl got to?

*(Evidently the balcony stretches along the length of the building.
PARTRIDGE, baffled and annoyed, sets off to find ASTRID,
disappearing in the opposite direction to that which we saw her
take. As he goes, we hear a key in the front door lock, and the front
door open. PROUT has let himself in, using the Embassy's spare
key, and now moves anxiously into the lounge, hoping that
MULLER's wife has not arrived yet. Looking round and seeing
no-one, he breathes a sigh of relief then PROUT notices the
balcony door is open. But there's no-one in sight out there so, ever
security-conscious, he closes the balcony door and draws the
curtains across. After which he crosses to the phone, picks up the
receiver, and dials.)*

PROUT. Hello, Kibble? ... Yes, luckily the Inspector was in a
hurry. I told him I knew nothing about Muller, and even less about his
currency case. Have you found out where Muller went? ... The
Mediterranean? Whereabouts – France, Spain, Italy? ... Well, that's no
good – find out exactly where he's staying – his travel agents may
know. Then book a ticket to the same place for his wife. First-class –
Americans like to travel in style. Hang the expense, the Government
pays, so it's only taxpayers' money. I'll camp outside this flat and
intercept her before she comes in. We'll keep her at the Embassy till
you find out where she's to go. Thank heaven she hasn't arrived yet ...

*(At this point, the bedroom door opens, and LADY PARTRIDGE
emerges, expecting to see her husband back.)*

GILLIAN. I've started my Pyrennees poem and I'm stuck for a
word ... oh!
PROUT. *(Shocked, to phone.)* My God, she *has* arrived! All right,
I'll cope and ring you back. *(PROUT puts the phone down quickly and
hurries to reassure the woman, who's as astonished to see PROUT as
he is shaken to see her.)* Ah, good evening, madame – please don't be
alarmed, I'm from the British Embassy. I didn't know you were here,
so I let myself in. We ... er ... have a key from your husband. Security,
and so on.
GILLIAN. My husband?
PROUT. I've a message for you from him.

GILLIAN. Oh yes, what is happening? My husband just flew off. He was worried about that case.

PROUT. Ah ... er ... you heard about the case. Just a misunderstanding, I'm sure. It'll all be sorted out. Er ... may I say, you don't *sound* American.

GILLIAN. *(Baffled)* Oh ... very kind of you to say so.

PROUT. The point is, there's been a change of plan. Your husband wants you to join him in the Mediterranean.

GILLIAN. Oh dear, I do wish he'd make up his mind. Still, I'll be quite happy to go there. We spent our honeymoon in the Mediterranean, you know.

PROUT. It's very pleasant there.

GILLIAN. I quite liked it, but I found it awfully hot.

PROUT. A lot of people like the heat.

GILLIAN. I suppose so. But I shall try and get them to turn it down.

PROUT. Er ... oh. I expect it'll be cooler anyway, being spring.

GILLIAN. And our room was such a long way from the dining-room. We had to go to the other end of the Mediterranean to eat.

PROUT. Pardon?

(The slight change of accommodation has now been displaced in LADY PARTRIDGE's mind by the more important matter of her poem.)

GILLIAN. Are you any good with words?

PROUT. Words?

GILLIAN. I've started a poem on the Pyrennees ... "Oh centuries-old stone, formed in primeval night, Womb-symbol of the world, giver of endless ..." *what,* d'you think?

PROUT. "Fright"?

GILLIAN. Yes, yes! No. No, that would rhyme, you see. We can't have that, it's a poem.

PROUT. Er ... your husband would like you with him as soon as possible. Perhaps I could help you get your things together. *(Anxious to get the woman out of the flat, PROUT opens the door of the bedroom from which she emerged and ushers her in.)* We have to go to the Embassy first – some formalities to complete.

GILLIAN. Yes, yes ... I thought of "lethargy" – that's a good tactile word, isn't it?

PROUT. Oh very. Let's discuss it while you're packing.

(PROUT has now got LADY PARTRIDGE into the bedroom. He follows her in and closes the door behind them. Now, once again, we hear a key in the lock and the front-door open. This is LOUISE MULLER, wife of MAX, returning home. She is an attractive, rather hard-boiled American in her late twenties. She enters the lounge, puts down her modest suitcase, goes to the drink cabinet and pours herself a vodka. Then she slumps into an easy-chair by the telephone, clearly at the end of a long journey. She picks up the receiver and dials, then drinks as she waits for an answer.)

LOUISE. Hi, Danielle, it's Louise Muller, I just got in ... Yeah, it was OK. Only Mom was on at me as usual... yeah, like always, when am I going to get rid of no-good Max, go home, settle down, find a nice wholesome Arab boy ... Yeah, well, that's no problem, Max has walked out on *me*. I had a cheque bounce, rang the Bank, Max had cleaned out our joint account, and was last seen heading South ... Listen, that guy's so crooked, when they bury him they'll need an L-shaped hole. I just wish they'd hurry up and do it! And he's got the morals of a stoat ... Yeah, I know I got a lover – but just one, Honey. Max does it with *groups* ... Can you speak up, I'm kinda deaf from the flight ... *(She hits the back of her head with her hand.)* ... No, I don't think it was the altitude, I guess it was the in-flight movie ... Yeah, The Towering Earthquake or some such ... No, I don't see Frou-Frou for ten days. He's got business, he's always got business. And a wife who can spot an affaire at twenty miles. We just meet once a month in Monaco – Frou-Frou's got a villa there Mrs. Frou-Frou doesn't know about. Listen, Danny, I'll see you tomorrow, I'm bushed, I gotta take a bath – we had boiler trouble. Max shoulda got plumbers in to fix it, but you can bet your ass he didn't ... Hell no, it's gonna be great to have this place to myself. Honey, you have no idea. I wouldn't have that bum back for all the rocks in Tiffany's. I'm writing Max right outta my life, anything he left in this flat goes straight down the rubbish chute – including his crummy clothes! ... Yeah, see you, Danny – take care. *(Her penultimate sentence was prompted by the sight of PARTRIDGE's suit on the chair. LOUISE replaces the phone receiver, then marches across and picks up the suit, together with the shirt.)* I don't remember this one, baby – guess this was for your society broads.

(With relish, LOUISE opens the door of the waste shredder, stuffs the clothes inside, and then closes the door again. Delighted with her deed, she dusts off her hands, and seeks a breath of fresh air. She pulls the balcony curtains open, and goes to open the balcony door. But, as PARTRIDGE found, the catch sometimes sticks. However, LOUISE is used to this, and deals it a swift karate chop with the side of her hand. Now the catch turns easily, and she slides the door open. She stands for a moment, breathing deeply. Then, leaving the balcony door open, she crosses and picks up her suitcase, and disappears into her bedroom [which, happily, is not the one LADY PARTRIDGE is using] to prepare for her bath. She closes her bedroom door behind her. Now PARTRIDGE comes back into view on the balcony, still baffled by ASTRID's disappearance. He steps into the room, leaving the balcony door open. At the same time, PROUT emerges from the other bedroom, carrying the suitcase belonging to the woman we know to be LADY PARTRIDGE, but who he thinks is MRS. MULLER. PROUT quickly shuts the bedroom door, and seeks a hiding-place for the suitcase among the furniture. PARTRIDGE is equally furtive.)

PROUT. Oh ... er ... you're here, sir. I let myself in with the Embassy key ... I thought you were out.

PARTRIDGE. No, no, I'm in. In fact, I'm here, as you say. Er ... have you seen my ... er ... doctor?

(Approaching the last word, PARTRIDGE remembers to clutch his back and assume a limp.)

PROUT. No ... no ... I thought perhaps she'd gone. *(The phone rings. Fortunately [since he wouldn't want the woman to hear it from the bedroom and come out] PROUT's search for a hiding-place for the suitcase has brought him close to the phone. He is able to pick it up instantly.)* Hello? ... oh, Kibble ... Monsieur Berri's arrived!? *(The news alarms both PROUT and PARTRIDGE, who each have a woman to hide. PROUT repeats the news as he hears it, in horror.)* The plane got in early? ... work to rule? ... guard-of-honour? ... *(Relief)* Oh, he's still at the airport? ... Yes, well, I'm glad. I'm not ... er ... Sir Clive's not ... quite ready to receive him yet. When he gets to the Embassy, look after him and ... er ... give us a ring before he comes over ... Yes, Sir Clive's with me. I'll deliver ... er ... that other item to you as soon as I can get her out ... er, get it out ... yes, quite. Thank you Kibble. *(PROUT hangs up, still in a state of alarm.)* Monsieur Berri's on his way to the Embassy, sir. He'll be coming here shortly.

PARTRIDGE. *(Stunned)* Yes ... yes ... my doctor ... perhaps she's gone ... *(He suddenly notices he's still in kimono and underwear.)* You said your man brought me new underwear and things. No time to have my suit cleaned, I'd better get it on ... my suit! Where is it?

(PARTRIDGE has recalled that his suit was on the chair. and now it's gone.)

PROUT. You dropped it, didn't you. And I picked it up and put it on that chair.

PARTRIDGE. Well, it's not there now. Who moved it?

PROUT. Not me, sir. It must have been your doctor.

PARTRIDGE. It was there two minutes ago. Since she went out on the balcony.

PROUT. Your doctor's out on the balcony?

PARTRIDGE. No! ... Yes! ... Well, possibly. She's a fresh-air fiend. Why are we rambling about my doctor? We've got to find my suit, man! We must search the flat!

PROUT. Must we? ... No, we can't ... I mean ...

PARTRIDGE. Don't stand there dithering! You're here to help me, aren't you?

(PARTRIDGE is striding towards his wife's bedroom, to start his search. PROUT believes the woman in there is MRS. MULLER, and he races PARTRIDGE to the door and blocks his entry.)

PROUT. All right, I'll look in here, sir – you have a look in the kitchen. *(PARTRIDGE hasn't time to argue, and hurries off to the kitchen. PROUT quickly opens the bedroom door.)* There isn't a man's suit in there, is there, Mrs. Muller? *(He stays blocking the doorway, and has a swift look inside.)* No, no, I thought not. Sorry to trouble you. *(Duty done, PROUT hurries out and shuts the door. He is puzzled. To himself.)* Perhaps she *did* take it out on the balcony ...

(PROUT walks out onto the balcony and disappears round the corner. As he does so, LADY PARTRIDGE emerges from her bedroom, looking baffled.)

GILLIAN. *(To herself.)* Mrs. Muller?

(But the lounge is empty, so LADY PARTRIDGE goes back in her room and shuts the door. PARTRIDGE, having looked in the kitchen, now comes out again. He is increasingly worried.)

PARTRIDGE. *(To himself.)* Perhaps she *did* take it out on the balcony ...

(PARTRIDGE walks out on the balcony and disappears in the same direction as PROUT. As he does so, LOUISE MULLER comes out of her bedroom, having removed her dress in preparation for her bath. She has a vague feeling she heard voices, and looks out on the balcony. Seeing no-one, she concludes that her ears are playing tricks. She hits the back of her head with her hand again, and disappears into the bathroom. Now PROUT and PARTRIDGE reappear on the balcony and come in through the balcony door.)

PARTRIDGE. No suit out there.
PROUT. And no doctor. Perhaps she went, and took your suit with her.
PARTRIDGE. Took my suit?! Why would she do that?
PROUT. I don't know, sir. Unless you over-looked one of her bills.

PARTRIDGE. Tchah! Did you look in both bedrooms?

PROUT. Oh ... no, I didn't.

PARTRIDGE. Well, let's see what's in here. *(The two men enter the bedroom LOUISE just left. It is empty, and we hear them talking, off, as they have a quick look round.)* Perhaps that old fool from the Embassy took it.

PROUT. Kibble? Oh, he wouldn't do a thing like that, sir. All our Embassy staff are totally reliable. Besides, it wouldn't fit him.

PARTRIDGE. Look in that cupboard! I tell you ... er ...

PROUT. Prout, sir.

PARTRIDGE. This whole visit has been totally mismanaged so far!

PROUT. You mustn't blame yourself, sir. We all have unlucky days. Nothing in here, sir.

PARTRIDGE. I wasn't blaming myself, man. Lost suitcases ... lost suits ... rumbling boilers ...

(The two men emerge from the bedroom, empty-handed.)

PROUT. Perhaps we should look in the dining-room.

PARTRIDGE. Very well ... but I can't think how it could be in there ...

(PROUT and PARTRIDGE march into the dining-room, and the spring-loaded door closes behind them. LOUISE emerges from the bathroom, carrying some cosmetics she had gone to fetch, walks briskly to her bedroom, goes in, and shuts the door. Then PROUT and PARTRIDGE come empty-handed from the dining-room.)

PARTRIDGE. It's incredible! It's vanished! How am I to receive Monsieur Berri? This could ruin my career, Prout!

PROUT. I think we've looked everywhere ... Ah! The bathroom!

PARTRIDGE. The bathroom?

PROUT. Well, it's worth a peep, sir. Or the hall? If you'll check those, I'll just look in this bedroom again.

PARTRIDGE. Oh very well.

(PARTRIDGE charges off into the bathroom and PROUT seizes the opportunity for a quick check on his problem woman. He opens the door of LADY PARTRIDGE's bedroom.)

PROUT. Are you nearly ready to leave, madame? *(PARTRIDGE comes out of the bathroom sooner than PROUT expected, and PROUT hastily shuts the bedroom door. PARTRIDGE goes out into the hall, and PROUT opens the bedroom door again.)* Just checking, no hurry, why don't you have a little rest there till I call you.

(PROUT shuts the bedroom door as PARTRIDGE returns in despair from the hall.)

PARTRIDGE. That's it, then. It's disappeared.

PROUT. Suits can't just disappear.

PARTRIDGE. My doctor *must* have moved it.

PROUT. Would she take it to the cleaners?

PARTRIDGE. Possibly. And me, if she had the chance.

PROUT. Pardon?

PARTRIDGE. Prout, there's only one thing for it!

PROUT. Sir?

PARTRIDGE. I'll have to borrow *your* suit.

PROUT. Well, of course if I ... what?! *My* suit? But my flat's on the other side of town, we'd never get back in time and ...

PARTRIDGE. Not your spare suit – *that* suit! The one you've got on! God knows, it's not up to much, but at least it'll cover my predicament.

PROUT. But ... but ... I mean ...

PARTRIDGE. No time to quibble, man, you said yourself the President of the Commerce Commission will be here any minute. Get that suit off and let me get it on!

PROUT. But I'm a third secretary! Third secretaries don't go round in underwear!

PARTRIDGE. The personal habits of third secretaries are no concern of mine. You're not meeting Monsieur Berri, I *am*! You can wear this wrap and stay out of the way while he's here. By the time he's gone, your bungling Embassy people might have found my suitcase.

PROUT. Wear the wrap? Me?

PARTRIDGE. Yes, you! Put the wrap on and wrap up! Here you are. *(PARTRIDGE slips off the kimono. He is wearing athletic vest and briefs underneath. He throws the kimono on a piece of furniture and advances on the unhappy PROUT.)* Come along, man, Britain's prestige in Europe is at stake! Get that suit off!

PROUT. But I can't ... I mean ... please ...

PARTRIDGE. Get that suit off!

(PROUT fears that PARTRIDGE's voice will bring his problem woman out of the bedroom. Reluctantly he accepts defeat.)

PROUT. All right, sir ... very well ... only please don't shout. I'll take my suit off in the other room ...

(PROUT hurries off into the dining-room.)

PARTRIDGE. I'm coming with you. I don't want you climbing out of the window and leaving me stranded!

(PARTRIDGE follows PROUT into the dining-room, and the spring-loaded door swings shut behind them. Now, LOUISE MULLER comes out of her bedroom again, thinking she's heard voices. But the lounge is empty. She goes out to look in the hall and, still seeing no-one, she shakes her head and hits the back of it with her hand. About to return to her bedroom, she spots the kimono where PARTRIDGE left it.)

LOUISE. Oh, we forgot our kimono, did we? We must have left in a hurry. Be nice not to have to see that again!

(LOUISE picks up the kimono, moves across and opens the door of the shredder, stuffs the kimono inside, closes the shredder door, and returns to her bedroom, closing the bedroom door behind her. Now PARTRIDGE comes out of the dining-room, still in vest and briefs, but carrying PROUT's suit. PROUT remains out of sight, holding the door open from within.)

PARTRIDGE. Good Lord, what a fuss! *(He puts down the jacket and measures the trousers against his legs.)* Never mind, these ought to fit. Shouldn't clash too badly with my shirt ... my shirt! Where's my shirt?

PROUT. I don't know, sir. Could you pass me the kimono, please?

PARTRIDGE. My shirt's gone! My shirt's disappeared with my suit!

PROUT. Could I have the kimono, Sir Clive?

PARTRIDGE. All in good time, Prout. First of all, I'm going to have to borrow your shirt.

PROUT. My shirt?

PARTRIDGE. Don't let's go through all that again! Just take off that shirt and give it to me!

(PARTRIDGE puts the trousers down beside the jacket and strides purposefully into the dining-room to acquire PROUT's shirt. The door swings shut behind them. Now LOUISE emerges from the bedroom to pour herself a drink. She catches sight of PROUT's suit, which PARTRIDGE put down somewhere she could have missed it before. She marches over and picks it up.)

LOUISE. You really did leave in a hurry, Max! This was your suit for conning the business boys, wasn't it? Well, time to give *this* the business!

(LOUISE carries the jacket and trousers to the shredder, opens the door and stuffs them inside. Pleased with her work, she closes the shredder door, goes to the drink cabinet, pours herself a drink, returns to the bedroom and shuts the door. After which the two men come out of the dining-room: PARTRIDGE now wearing PROUT's shirt over his vest and briefs: PROUT looking miserable, and seen for the first time in his rather more conservative underwear. PARTRIDGE goes to pick up PROUT's suit and put it on, but it's no longer there.)

PARTRIDGE. You just keep out of the way! Once I've got this suit on, I ... Good God!

PROUT. What is it, sir?

PARTRIDGE. *Your* suit's gone!

PROUT. *My* suit's gone?

PARTRIDGE. Yes, your suit has gone! Disappeared! I put it here! It's gone!

PROUT. But I lent you that suit in good faith! That's my best suit!

PARTRIDGE. Good grief, man, *I* haven't harmed it! *(He reluctantly accepts the only apparent explanation.) She* must have taken it!

PROUT. Your doctor?

PARTRIDGE. She did take my suit! And now she's taken yours!

PROUT. My suit didn't need cleaning! I had it done last year!

PARTRIDGE. Not for cleaning, man, for malice! A vendetta! It has to be her. There's no-one else ... is there?

PROUT. No ... no ... of course not. Did you upset her?

PARTRIDGE. She was cross, but I thought she'd got over it.

PROUT. Oh, the business with your pills.

PARTRIDGE. Er ... quite. What am I going to do, Prout? Berri's coming here and I've got no clothes! What the hell am I going to do?

PROUT. I don't know, sir. This didn't come up in our Foreign Office lectures.

PARTRIDGE. This could change the history of Europe! I shall be a laughing-stock, someone else'll get the Presidency – probably that pushy little man from Israel!

PROUT. Israel isn't in the Common Market.

PARTRIDGE. They aren't in Europe, but that didn't stop them winning the Eurovision Song Contest. This is a dark day for Britain, Prout. Our trade at risk ... our prestige in jeopardy ... and ... and ...

PROUT. And I'm rather cold.

(The evening air has been getting to PROUT in his underwear. He shuts the balcony door.)

PARTRIDGE. That fellow you're renting from – did he leave any clothes behind?

PROUT. He can't have done. We'd have seen them when we searched the flat.

PARTRIDGE. So there are no clothes here at all?

PROUT. Seems not, sir.

PARTRIDGE. Well, ring someone at the Embassy. That old fool who was here earlier.

PROUT. Kibble? He went off to meet Monsieur Berri. Wait! That parcel Kibble brought! It's supposed to be socks and underwear, but it looks a bit bulky. Perhaps he picked up some slacks as well.

PARTRIDGE. Slacks? This is a formal meeting!

PROUT. Slacks would be better than nothing ... *(PROUT has hurried across the room to KIBBLE's parcel and is now wrestling with the knot, which he can't untie. He tries easing the string round the end of the parcel, but it won't go.)* Monsieur Berri might think it was this year's fashion.

PARTRIDGE. Well, come on – open it, man!

PROUT. It won't undo ...

PARTRIDGE. Well, tear the paper!

PROUT. I'd rather not, sir. The Ambassador is very against wasting paper. There may be some scissors in the kitchen.

(PROUT picks up the parcel and hurries off to the kitchen. PARTRIDGE remains alone in the lounge, showing symptoms of mounting paranoia.)

PARTRIDGE. My God, what have I done to deserve this? *(Now ASTRID reappears round the corner on the balcony, with her dress torn and trellis round her shoulders. PARTRIDGE sees her, leaps up and rushes to the balcony door to let her in, but the lock has jammed again. He wrestles with it, at the same time interrogating ASTRID in an urgent whisper through the ventilator.)* Where the devil have you been!? What the hell are you doing?!

ASTRID. I was trying to climb to the roof – you could not open the door – it seemed the only way!

PARTRIDGE. But I opened the door!

ASTRID. Well, open it again!

PARTRIDGE. I can't!

ASTRID. So it *was* the only way. But the flowers would not hold me. I have bruised my bottom.

PARTRIDGE. I'll bruise your bottom when I get hold of you! Have you got my suit?

ASTRID. Your suit? Of course I have not got your suit! And why are you undressed? Have you got a woman in there?

PARTRIDGE. Is that all you can think of!? ... This blasted window ...

(As PARTRIDGE struggles, PROUT rushes excitedly from the kitchen. ASTRID, conscious of her torn dress, hides behind the shrub.)

PROUT. Sir Clive! Sir Clive! There are trousers in the parcel! Well, sort of.

PARTRIDGE. Thank God for that! What d'you mean 'sort of'?

PROUT. Kibble brought the wrong package! He's left us some costumes for Yeomen of the Guard!

PARTRIDGE. Yeomen of the Guard?

PROUT. The Embassy Players! *(A horrid thought strikes him.)* Oh dear. That means two Yeomen will go onstage in your underwear!

PARTRIDGE. Never mind that! You say, we've got trousers?

PROUT. They're not exactly trousers, they're the sort of things Yeomen wear.

PARTRIDGE. Good grief, man, don't stand there rambling, show me! I've got to open this damn door!

PROUT. Why, sir?

PARTRIDGE. Why? ... Why? ... because I need fresh air! Get the trousers, for God's sake! *(PROUT hurries back into the kitchen. PARTRIDGE delves in the toolbag which has been lying there unobtrusively. He finds the screwdriver and resumes his battle with the lock and his whispered conversation with ASTRID. She is peering round her shrub.)* If you haven't got my suit, where is it?

ASTRID. I don't know anything about your suit.

PARTRIDGE. You started all this trouble. You shouldn't have come here!

ASTRID. I wish I hadn't!

PARTRIDGE. Keep your voice down! My wife is resting in that bedroom!

(PROUT emerges from the kitchen, wearing his vest plus Yeomen of the Guard trousers. These resemble red tights. ASTRID hides. PARTRIDGE is appalled.)

PROUT. These are the trousers, sir!

PARTRIDGE. Good Lord! You look like a septic finger!

PROUT. It's all we've got. Two pairs of these, and two funny tunic things.

PARTRIDGE. I'm not wearing those to meet Jacques Berri! I'd sooner wear the kimono! *(PARTRIDGE discovers the kimono is no longer where he put it.)* The kimono's gone! Am I going mad?

(The phone starts to ring: but, again, PROUT is able to pick it up instantly.)

PROUT. Hello ... Kibble?

PARTRIDGE. My God! Berri's here!

(PARTRIDGE dives into the kitchen.)

PROUT. Yes, of course it's me! ... What? ... Monsieur Berri's gone to the German consulate? Thank heavens! ... just a courtesy call, I see ... still, that's got to be forty minutes, those Germans are awfully courteous when they're roused ... Ah, you've found out where Muller went! ... It *was* the Mediterranean? ... Cannes, I see ... Buy Mrs. Muller's ticket at once, and I'll get her over to the Embassy ... Well done! Stay close to Berri and keep us posted ... Thank you, Kibble ... *(PROUT is about to hang up when he remembers their other problem.)* Oh Kibble, this is urgent, can you get us some cl ... hello, Kibble? ... Kibble? Oh Lord, he's gone.

(PARTRIDGE now comes out of the kitchen, in vest, red tights and a panic.)

PARTRIDGE. Is Berri on his way? How long have we got?

PROUT. About forty minutes, sir. Monsieur Berri's making a courtesy call on the Germans. Kibble is with him.

PARTRIDGE. That's a relief – then there's time to get some proper clothes. Ring someone, Prout! Ring your secretary!

PROUT. I'll try, sir. She may still be at the office, the Conference has made extra work for everyone ... *(PROUT starts to dial.)* She isn't very bright, I'm afraid. She made rather a hash of the visa section, so they promoted her to my office.

PARTRIDGE. I don't want to hear the absurd politics of your incompetent Embassy, I just want some clothes! Apart from looking ridiculous, these trousers are damned uncomfortable!

PROUT. You've got them back-to-front, sir. Your you-know's where your whatsit should be, and your whatsit's the wrong way round.

PARTRIDGE. Aaaaaaagh!

(PARTRIDGE storms off to the kitchen to change his tights round. PROUT's secretary has answered.)

PROUT. Hello, Miss Jellicoe, Simon Prout here ... no, it's not about the biscuit money, it's rather unusual ... Actually, you see, the thing is, I'm here with Sir Clive Partridge and we've got no clothes ... No, Miss Jellicoe, this isn't an obscene phone call ... Yes, of course it's me! Look, it's perfectly simple, if you must know. Sir Clive made me take my trousers off ... he's already *seen* a doctor! It was she who pinched his things ... Look, Miss Jellicoe, please don't argue. I want you to go at once to my flat ... No, of course I shan't be there! The key's on the ledge in the corridor behind the rubber plant ... Go into my bedroom ... no, no, I won't tell anyone ... get the two suits from the wardrobe and bring them here to Mrs. Muller's flat ... take a taxi there and a taxi here ... Yes, of course it's Embassy business. Britain's place in Europe is at stake. Now please get on with it!

(PROUT replaces the receiver and pauses for breath. As he does so, LADY PARTRIDGE opens her bedroom door and stands in the doorway. PROUT is terrified that PARTRIDGE will come from the kitchen and see her.)

GILLIAN. I'm almost ready to leave, I just want to finish this poem. I may not get the same vibrations in the Mediterranean Hotel.

PROUT. No, quite – no hurry. You go back in there and lie down.

GILLIAN. I'm looking for a word that doesn't rhyme with "moon". *(She notices PROUT's curious clothing.)* Er ... why are you wearing red tights?

PROUT. Tights ... tights ... these aren't tights – they're ... er ... athletics gear. The Ambassador likes all his staff to jog. I was just having a little jog around the flat. Tell you what, I'll jog into the bedroom and help you with your word ...

(PROUT high-steps towards the bedroom, causing LADY PARTRIDGE to retreat therein. PROUT follows her, and shuts the door behind them. As he does so, PARTRIDGE comes back from the kitchen with his tights adjusted. ASTRID is in view on the balcony, looking bewildered. PARTRIDGE hurries across and resumes his attempt to let her in, attacking the lock with the screwdriver again, and nagging ASTRID through the ventilator.)

ASTRID. Hurry up, please – I'm cold, Poochy!

PARTRIDGE. Don't call me that! You storm in here just before a critical meeting ... you jam this lock ... you come and go and then appear again like a dose of toothache! I'm doing my b ... Aaaagh!

(The screwdriver has slipped and caught PARTRIDGE's hand. He dances with pain and rage.)

ASTRID. Poochy, be quiet! Your wife is resting in the bedroom there!

PARTRIDGE. I've gashed my finger, thanks to you! This is going to bleed ... you know how I bleed when I gash myself!

ASTRID. You do not have to be such a bleeder. Hold it under the cold tap ... that will stop it!

PARTRIDGE. Yes, the cold tap ... tch, this on top of everything! Look, for God's sake stay out of sight!

ASTRID. Yes, Poochy ... sorry, Poochy ...

(ASTRID goes back behind her shrub. PARTRIDGE picks up the toolbag and hurries off to the bathroom. But as soon as he's in there, and turns on the tap, the boiler starts to rumble. Alarmed,

PARTRIDGE comes out of the bathroom. He has turned the tap off, but the boiler will rumble on for some seconds. PARTRIDGE has left the toolbag in the bathroom and has wet hands, having failed to find a towel. He moves toward the kitchen to find a towel and silence the boiler. On the way he pulls the cord to close the balcony curtains, to be on the safe side. Then he disappears into the kitchen.)

(LOUISE comes out of her bedroom, wearing a towelling wrap, and disquieted by the boiler rumble. She moves towards the kitchen, but before she gets there the rumble stops. She shrugs and turns to go to the bathroom, but sees the balcony curtains are closed. Thinking she must have absent-mindedly pulled them across, she now pulls the cord to open them before disappearing into the bathroom.)

(PARTRIDGE comes out of the kitchen, still with wet hands and muttering to himself.)

PARTRIDGE. No towels in the bathroom, no towels in the kitchen ... where *are* the blasted towels?

(PARTRIDGE sees the curtains are opened and, assuming he failed to close them, he now does so. Then he enters the bedroom which LOUISE just left. As he disappears, LOUISE comes out of the bathroom with the toolbag and a surprised look. She is in her briefs, having discarded her towelling wrap in the bathroom. She was about to run the bath when she discovered the toolbag: which she is now returning to its proper place in the kitchen. As she crosses the stage, she notices the balcony curtains are closed and, thinking she must have forgotten to open them as she intended, she does so before disappearing into the kitchen.)

(PARTRIDGE comes out of the bedroom, having failed to find a towel. But his hands are almost dry, and he proposes to get on with attacking the lock. He's surprised to find he failed to close the balcony curtains as he intended, and closes them now. Then he goes into the bathroom to get his toolbag. He is astonished to find it isn't there: but agreeably surprised to discover what he takes to be a towel: and emerges drying his hands on what is, in fact, LOUISE's towelling wrap.)

PARTRIDGE. I could have sworn I left the toolbag there ... where else was I? ... bedroom?

(PARTRIDGE goes back into the bedroom he recently left, to seek his toolbag. As he does so, LOUISE comes from the kitchen, having left the toolbag there. As she crosses the lounge, she opens the curtains: then proceeds to the bathroom for her bath, goes in, and shuts the door.)
(PROUT comes out of the other bedroom, carrying LADY PARTRIDGE's empty sherry glass, and calling back to her in the room.)

PROUT. Yes, I'm sure there's more sherry – I saw another bottle in the cabinet.

(Noticing the curtains are open, PROUT closes them. Then he goes to the drinks cabinet, fills the glass with sherry, and takes it back to LADY PARTRIDGE's bedroom.)
(Still seeking his toolbag, PARTRIDGE emerges from the other bedroom and crosses to the kitchen. As he passes the balcony, he automatically pulls the curtain cord: a few paces further on, he stops, puzzled. He has realized he opened the curtains, instead of closing them, as formerly. He goes back and closes the curtains, then carries on into the kitchen to find his toolbag. To his surprise, PARTRIDGE finds his toolbag in the kitchen, and he emerges carrying it. He goes to the balcony door, opens the curtains, signals to ASTRID to lie low and be quiet, and tackles the lock once again with the screwdriver. After a moment's effort, he succeeds, and slides the door open. He looks furtively round and, finding the coast clear, beckons urgently to ASTRID to make her escape at last.)

PARTRIDGE. Quick! Quick, for heaven's sake, now's your chance!

(ASTRID darts out from behind her shrub, and is almost into the room when a bedroom door opens and LADY PARTRIDGE comes out,

speaking over her shoulder to PROUT – who follows closely behind her, anxious to stop her wandering round the flat. PARTRIDGE panics at the thought of his wife seeing ASTRID. He dashes out onto the balcony, bundles ASTRID behind her shrub, and hides there with her.)

GILLIAN. I'm afraid this sherry is much too dry – it's like drinking skin freshener.

PROUT. I'm sure we could find you something more pleasant at the Embassy. Shall we go straight there now?

GILLIAN. No, my throat is parched, I must have a drink of water. The kitchen is over here, is it? I wish you could find me some aspirin – this headache won't go.

(LADY PARTRIDGE disappears into the kitchen, and PROUT looks anxiously for aspirins. Noticing the balcony door is open, he closes it. Then he spots ASTRID's tablet bottle, picks it up, and calls after LADY PARTRIDGE in the kitchen.)

PROUT. These aren't aspirins, but they're pain-killers. Very effective, I believe. A couple of these should solve your problems.

(LADY PARTRIDGE having turned the tap on, the kitchen boiler starts to rumble. PROUT follows LADY PARTRIDGE into the kitchen to try and help. With the lounge empty, PARTRIDGE and ASTRID rush to the balcony door, but it won't open from the outside. They dash back and hide again, as LADY PARTRIDGE emerges from the kitchen with her glass of water, and PROUT in attendance. The boiler noise is dying down.)

GILLIAN. What on earth is the matter? I simply turned on the cold tap and the boiler began to belch.

PROUT. I'm afraid this plumbing is rather suspect. It's lucky you're off to the Mediterranean. Let's get across to the Embassy at once. They've arranged everything.

GILLIAN. But there's water all over the kitchen floor. We can't leave it like that.

PROUT. Can't we? No, all right, I'll mop it up.

GILLIAN. And the boiler is trembling with rage.

PROUT. I'll see if I can fix it. You take your tablets and then you'll be ready to go. You'll have no more worries.

GILLIAN. Yes, I must say, I'll be glad to say goodbye to all this. *(She notices the balcony curtains are open.)* I'll just draw these curtains – my husband likes them closed. He doesn't want the sunshine to spoil the furniture.

(LADY PARTRIDGE closes the curtains and goes back into her bedroom with her tablets and glass, shutting the door behind her. PROUT has gone into the kitchen, but quickly emerges.)

PROUT. There's no floor-cloth. *(He discovers that LADY PARTRIDGE has returned to the bedroom and he is talking to himself. He shrugs.)* Floor-cloth ... floor-cloth ... bathroom, perhaps? *(PROUT crosses the stage, opens the bathroom door, and marches briskly in. There is a scream from LOUISE, a cloud of steam, and PROUT recoils, aghast.)* I say, I'm most awfully sorry ... oh dear ... I didn't know ...

(An angry LOUISE follows him out, covered only with a bathmat on which the word "BIENVENUE" is emblazoned. She wields as a potential weapon a fish-shaped back-brush. PROUT boggles.)

LOUISE. Who the hell are you, and what are you doing here?

PROUT. I'm terribly sorry, I didn't realize you were there ... I wanted the floor-cloth ... I'm trying to mend the boiler, you see ...

LOUISE. Mend the boiler? Oh I see. *(LOUISE assumes he's a plumber and puts down her brush on a handy surface.)* Well, thank God for that! So my husband *did* get someone to fix it! You got the key from the porter, I suppose?

PROUT. Your *husband?* *(He assumes this is LADY PARTRIDGE.)* Ah, I see – I didn't know you'd arrived.

LOUISE. Well, of course I've arrived! I had a hell of a flight, I'm tired, and I want a rest! So will you please stay out of my bathroom and get on and fix that goddam boiler! *(LOUISE returns to the bathroom and shuts the door behind her. But, almost at once, she opens it again and sticks her head out.)* And who keeps closing those goddam curtains? Will you please open them and keep them open!

(LOUISE disappears and closes the bathroom door again. As instructed, PROUT crosses to the balcony curtains and opens them. This reveals the anxious faces of PARTRIDGE and ASTRID peering in. PARTRIDGE whispers urgently to PROUT through the ventilator.)

PARTRIDGE. Quick, man, for God's sake open this door! You may have to lever it with something from the toolbag!

(PROUT finds the screwdriver and gets to work.)

PROUT. So you found your doctor, Sir Clive. Is she all right? She looks rather vandalized.

PARTRIDGE. Doctor? ... Oh yes, never mind that ... get on with it, man!

PROUT. And I see your wife's arrived, sir.

PARTRIDGE. Yes, yes, she's been here a while. She's resting in the bedroom.

PROUT. Ah, got it. *(PROUT has slipped the catch, and slides the door open.)* Come on in, sir.

PARTRIDGE. *(Warily)* My wife *is* in the bedroom, I take it?

PROUT. No sir, she's taking a bath. I'm afraid I burst in on her, not knowing she was there.

PARTRIDGE. *(Relieved)* A bath? Excellent! The coast's clear, dear ... I mean, dear doctor.

(PARTRIDGE and ASTRID come in from the balcony.)

PROUT. Don't you want your wife to see your doctor?

PARTRIDGE. No! No, she has a morbid fear of doctors.

PROUT. Really?

PARTRIDGE. Medicophobia, they call it. She had an unhappy experience while watching Dr. Finlay's Casebook. *(He chivvies ASTRID.)* Come along, my dear, no time to lose. Go, quickly!

ASTRID. Au revoir, Poochy. Sorry about my silly suspicions.
PROUT. Suspicions?
PARTRIDGE. You remember, she thought I'd skipped my pills.

(As the three stand by the balcony, the bathroom door opens and LOUISE and a cloud of steam emerge. LOUISE is concerned only to retrieve her back-brush – which she does quickly without seeing the trio. LOUISE returns to the bathroom and shuts the door behind her. PARTRIDGE is amazed at the appearance of this strange woman: and ASTRID is instantly hostile.)

ASTRID. That is your wife? You said your wife was plain! This woman is very sexy!
PARTRIDGE. That woman is *not* my wife!
ASTRID. Not your wife? Then who is this naked woman, bathing in your flat?
PROUT. One moment, doctor. Sir Clive must have been confused by the steam. That *is* his wife.
PARTRIDGE. What?
ASTRID. I hope so. I told you already, Poochy – your wife, all right. But a third woman, no! I would kill you! Now, you swear that is your wife?
PARTRIDGE. Just a minute, I need time to think ...
PROUT. Of course that's your wife, sir. I was talking to her just a moment ago.
PARTRIDGE. *(Taking the plunge.)* Yes, yes, of course that *is* my wife – I just didn't recognize her with her clothes off. Now I think about it, I realize that *is* my wife. Absolutely. Now you run along, my dear. There's no third woman in my life.

(Now the bedroom door opens, and LADY PARTRIDGE comes out – looking her best for arrival at a new hotel, and carrying the tablet bottle, which she puts down. She is surprised to see her husband.)

GILLIAN. I can't get the top off this bottle ... Clive darling, you're here! I was waiting in the bedroom for you!
ASTRID. What?! Who is this?!

GILLIAN. I'm so looking forward to our stay in the Mediterranean. I just thought I'd better take a pill.

ASTRID. So! There is no third woman in your life! You Bluebeard! You randy English philatelist! I will fix you!

(The enraged ASTRID picks up a vase and swings it at PARTRIDGE's head. PARTRIDGE ducks and ASTRID hits the bemused PROUT instead. PROUT slumps to the floor as the curtain falls.)

A RISE IN THE MARKET

ACT II

(The curtain rises on the same scene, five minutes later. PROUT has been moved onto a settee, where he now lies unconscious. LADY PARTRIDGE and ASTRID hover in attendance, the latter aghast at her deed. PARTRIDGE is postponing awkward questions by adopting a masterful manner, and focussing all attention on the plight of the injured man. He sits on the settee by PROUT's head, and studies his face for signs of life. Both men are still in their vests and red Yeomen of the Guard tight trousers.)

GILLIAN. Clive, I don't understand what's going on. Who is this gir ...

PARTRIDGE. No time for questions, my dear – a man is injured, perhaps dying. We need brandy.

GILLIAN. I'd be sick, I'll stick to sherry.

PARTRIDGE. Not for you, for him. Get some brandy, quick.

GILLIAN. There's none in the cabinet, I looked earlier.

PARTRIDGE. Go to the British Embassy – it's just across the road.

GILLIAN. Across the road?

PARTRIDGE. The porter downstairs will show you. Tell them who you are, and ask for a First Aid kit and a bottle of brandy!

GILLIAN. I'll get some sherry as well – that bottle's almost empty.

PARTRIDGE. All right, Gillian, but go! Go now!

GILLIAN. Very well, Clive, if you think that's best.

(LADY PARTRIDGE exits to the hall, and we hear the front door close behind her.)

ASTRID. Poochy, I did not mean to hit him – you know that!

PARTRIDGE. No, you meant to hit me, you wicked girl. It's the same in law. You meant to cause grievous bodily harm, and you did!

ASTRID. I was confused. Who are these women – if that's your wife, who is the girl in the bathroom?

PARTRIDGE. Never mind that – your victim's in a bad way! Get in the kitchen and boil some water!

ASTRID. Boil water? What for?

PARTRIDGE. Don't you go to the cinema? When a baby's born, or someone's hurt, boiling water's essential!

ASTRID. But Poochy ...

PARTRIDGE. Don't argue, just do as I say. You could find yourself on a manslaughter charge!

ASTRID. Is he dead?

PARTRIDGE. He might be, he's looking awful. Mind you, he looked pretty awful before you hit him. But he's scarcely breathing.

ASTRID. Oh Poochy, will they arrest me? What shall I do?

PARTRIDGE. Go and boil some water, like I said.

ASTRID. What shall I do when I've boiled the water?

PARTRIDGE. Well ... er ... cut some sandwiches.

ASTRID. All right, Poochy ... don't let him die!

(ASTRID, in a state of shock, exits to the kitchen. PROUT is beginning to stir. He opens his eyes and groans.)

PROUT. Why did your doctor hit me?

PARTRIDGE. My doctor? ... er ... hit you? Ah ... er ... she thought you were going to have hysterics.

PROUT. But I wasn't doing anything.

PARTRIDGE. Exactly. One of the surest signs. My doctor thinks prevention's better than cure.

(PROUT sits up, now wide awake.)

PROUT. I don't believe that woman is a doctor.

PARTRIDGE. Good Lord! You think she's been fooling me all this time?

PROUT. No, I think you've been fooling me. And your wife. That woman called you Poochy. And she was jealous! I think she's your lover!

PARTRIDGE. Lover? You'd better rest, you're delirious!

PROUT. I can find out, you know.

PARTRIDGE. Don't you pry into my affairs, you insolent oaf! I'll get you kicked out of the Foreign Service!

PROUT. I've only to ask your wife who your doctor is.

PARTRIDGE. My wife? ... my dear chap, look, you and I are friends, aren't we?

PROUT. Are we?

PARTRIDGE. Of course we are. I liked you the moment we met. I thought, there's a young man who'll go to the top ... with the right backing. He's discreet, a man of the world, a true diplomat.

PROUT. Oh. D'you think so?

PARTRIDGE. I'm sure of it. And this is your chance to show how diplomatic you are.

PROUT. Really?

PARTRIDGE. And you're bright, too. Of course, you're right about Astrid. She's not a doctor. I suppose she *is* a sort of lover, in a way.

PROUT. What sort of way?

PARTRIDGE. Er ... whichever way we fancy. I'm kept apart from my wife for long periods, in the service of the nation. Astrid was besotted with me, you don't want to hurt a young girl's feelings ... and there you have it.

PROUT. *Where* d'you have it?

PARTRIDGE. Oh ... Brussels, Rome, Bonn ... I mean it was inevitable. We've been discreet – no-one's suffered.

PROUT. I'm suffering. I've got toothache all over my head.

PARTRIDGE. A misunderstanding. No-one's suffered in the past. It's up to us to see no-one suffers in the future.

PROUT. Us?

PARTRIDGE. Me ... and *you*!

PROUT. Me?

PARTRIDGE. Keep quiet about what you know. We have to see no-one else finds out, Prout!

PROUT. But your wife ...

PARTRIDGE. Especially my wife. And Monsieur Berri. If he knew, my election chances would be up the spout, Prout!

PROUT. You want me to conceal you illicit affaire?

PARTRIDGE. Exactly – I said you were bright! We have to get

Astrid out of here, without anyone knowing she happened. My wife mustn't know and Monsieur Berri mustn't know. I've got to win that election tomorrow! For Britain, Prout, for all the little people at home. You know what it means if I'm elected President! I'll be one of the top men in Brussels, Prout! For the British, there'll be the leadership of Europe! For you there'll be a glittering diplomatic career ...

PROUT. And for you, more birds on the side!

PARTRIDGE. And for me, more b ... Prout, how dare you!

PROUT. I'm sorry, Sir Clive, but it's no part of my duties to cover up scandal. If I helped you through this mess, it could boost my career. I might get to the top, make a lot of money. But I couldn't live with myself.

PARTRIDGE. If you make a lot of money, you can live with who you like!

PROUT. I believe public figures should set an example. Call me a narrow-minded prig, of you like ...

PARTRIDGE. You're a narrow-minded prig! And a damn stupid one, too! A fellow Englishman in trouble, and you won't help! Well, one day you'll be in trouble and then the boot'll be on the other side of your face! You disgust me, Prout! You're a stupid, bungling, obstinate ... (*The kitchen door opens and ASTRID comes out. To maintain the fiction that PROUT is seriously ill, PARTRIDGE instantly pushes him flat and holds his shoulders down on the sofa.*) You poor chap, you're in a bad way. Don't try to move.

ASTRID. The kettle's boiled. What do you want me to do with it?

PARTRIDGE. Kettle? That's all you've done? We need more hot water than that! Boil a couple of saucepans as well.

ASTRID. But Poochy ...

PARTRIDGE. Don't argue, woman, this man's at death's door. Get on with it!

(*ASTRID shrugs and returns to the kitchen, closing the door behind her. As PARTRIDGE relaxes his grip, PROUT is able to struggle upright again. PARTRIDGE glares at him.*)

PROUT. Why can't she get hot water from the bathroom?

PARTRIDGE. Because there's a woman in there, isn't there! (*A thought strikes him.*) Just a minute, who *is* that woman?

PROUT. What?

PARTRIDGE. The woman in the bathroom – who is she?

PROUT. That's your wife. Just arrived. Had a bad flight. Threatened me with a back-brush. Haven't you met her?

PARTRIDGE. Met her?

PROUT. Well, of course, you must have met her to have married her – I mean, haven't you met her since she arrived? It *is* your wife – you said so to your doctor ... well, your lover ... only you didn't recognize her at first because of the steam. Didn't recognize your wife, that is, not your doctor ... lover ...

PARTRIDGE. Cut it out, Prout! My wife is the lady who came from the bedroom, the lady who has now gone to the Embassy to get you some brandy ...

PROUT. I don't drink brandy.

PARTRIDGE. If she brings brandy, you'll drink brandy! That is my wife! The woman in the bathroom I've never seen before! Who is she?

PROUT. If she's not your wife, I don't know who she is.

PARTRIDGE. You don't know who she is? You rented this flat on behalf of the Embassy! You're responsible for it! Is there a strange woman living here?

PROUT. No, of course not ... oh my God ... goodness ...

(PROUT has realized he was trying to evict the wrong woman. His head slumps back on the sofa. PARTRIDGE yanks him upright again.)

PARTRIDGE. Pull yourself together, man! What the devil's going on?

PROUT. I've got the pains again.

PARTRIDGE. You *know* that woman in the bathroom! I suppose she's *your* bit of crumpet – your very own diplomatic bag!

PROUT. Certainly not! I don't ... I mean, I've never ... look, Sir Clive, there may have been a slight misunderstanding ... it's just struck me ...

PARTRIDGE. Get on with it, or *I'll* strike you!

PROUT. It seems there was a small oversight in the lease. That woman doesn't actually live here, but she is entitled to, well, visit ... as a visitor ... visiting. Well, more than that, really ... in a way she's entitled to stay a short while ... well, quite a long while, really ... actually, as long as she likes. If I'm going to be absolutely honest, she *does* live here ... well, to tell the truth, she owns the place. I rented it from her husband, and he wasn't entitled to let it.

PARTRIDGE. You incompetent buffoon! You've bungled this whole business! The Ambassador will nullify your credentials!

PROUT. I'm sorry, sir.

PARTRIDGE. I'll get you fired from the Foreign Service! When this story gets out, they'll have you shovelling slate for the Coal Board!

PROUT. Just a minute, Sir Clive. If this story gets out, we'll *both* be in trouble. People are going to hear about your girl friend.

PARTRIDGE. I thought that was what you wanted.

PROUT. I've had second thoughts, sir. You see, I'm arranging for Mrs. Muller to join her husband in the Mediterranean. If we help each other, we can get her out of here, and your girl friend, before Monsieur Berri arrives.

PARTRIDGE. Well, that' a different story. You mean, we *will* do a cover-up?

PROUT. I see now you have to win that election. For Britain. It's my duty to help.

PARTRIDGE. I'm glad to hear it. Now listen – Astrid's terrified because she hit you. You must act seriously injured, so I can frighten her off.

PROUT. I have to act injured?

PARTRIDGE. Seriously injured. So I can scare Astrid away. If you've got that in your head, you have it in a nut-shell.

PROUT. But how can I act seriously injured? Mrs. Muller thinks I'm a plumber.

PARTRIDGE. What?

PROUT. Mrs. Muller, sir. The girl in the bath. She thinks I'm a plumber ... Oh my God ... goodness ...

(The bathroom door has opened and LOUISE has come out. She is amazed to see there are now two strangely-clad men in her lounge, and that they are huddled together on the sofa.)

LOUISE. What the hell is going on here?

PROUT. Er ... hello, madame. I had a little accident while working on the boiler. My colleague suggested I lie down for a moment.

LOUISE. Colleague?

PROUT. This job needed two men. He's a plumber's mate – aren't you, sir ... sir ... certainly he is.

PARTRIDGE. How d'you do, madame. We'll get her fixed in no time, don't you worry ... er, cor blimey.

LOUISE. Why are you wearing that fancy gear?

PARTRIDGE. Er ... Common Market regulations. We're Europlumbers. This is the new uniform. Strewth.

LOUISE. How come my husband gets Europlumbers? Why not just the local guys?

PROUT. Oh, we are local, Mrs. Muller. But we belong to the European Union. It helps us offer a better service. For special occasions, you can telegraph plumbing anywhere in Europe.

PARTRIDGE. That's right. You can order a bath for Barcelona ...

PROUT. ... or a sink for Helsinki ...

PARTRIDGE. ... or two loos for Toulouse!

LOUISE. Well, if you're local guys, how d'you get to speak English so well?

PARTRIDGE. Ah ... er ... we've spent a lot of time in England.

PROUT. The Europlumbers' Exchange Scheme. English plumbers come over here ...

PARTRIDGE. And we go over there!

LOUISE. *(Incredulous)* Europlumbers' Exchange Scheme? Where in England were you plumbing?

PARTRIDGE. Er ... in the Bath area.

LOUISE. I guess I still got jet-lag. *(She hits the back of her head with the side of her hand again.)* I gotta rest up a bit. If the phone rings, or the door, you guys take messages, will you? And, Lover – for Pete's sake get that boiler fixed. Otherwise we better call Super-Plumber!

(LOUISE exits to the bedroom and shuts the door.)

PARTRIDGE. You say you can get that woman out of here?

PROUT. Muller fled to the Mediterranean. Mr. Kibble from the

Embassy is getting her a ticket to the same place. He'll say her husband sent for her.

PARTRIDGE. But Berri will be here any minute!

PROUT. I'll worry about Mrs. Muller, you worry about your girl friend!

PARTRIDGE. I'll get rid of Astrid now, if you can act unconscious.

PROUT. Unconscious?

PARTRIDGE. I told you I have to scare her, say you might die. I'll tell her that if she gets away fast, I can pretend it was an accident. I've got to put a bomb under her.

(There is a short sharp non-recurring bang from the boiler, and ASTRID comes running out of the kitchen. Her face and dress are covered in soot. PARTRIDGE forces PROUT flat on the sofa.)

ASTRID. Poochy, the boiler has vomited!

PARTRIDGE. I'm afraid we have an emergency here. A traumatic coma.

ASTRID. I don't care what kind of boiler it is! It has banged me in the kitchen!

PARTRIDGE. Damn the boiler, woman! This man you hit may not survive!

ASTRID. *(Noticing the soot on her dress.)* My God, what am I going to do?

PARTRIDGE. Get out and leave it to me! I'll say it was an accident – he fell and hit his head. But you must leave at once!

ASTRID. I cannot leave here with soot on my dress! *(She touches her face.)* And on my face also! I cannot expose myself like this!

PARTRIDGE. You'd rather stay, and face a manslaughter charge?

ASTRID. I will wash my face and sponge my dress. Then we shall see.

PARTRIDGE. But Astrid ... listen ...

(ASTRID goes to the bathroom in a bad temper and shuts the door behind her. PARTRIDGE has risen and taken a few steps towards her in vain. PROUT sits upright.)

PROUT. She's not going to go.

PARTRIDGE. I don't think she is. Hell, what if she's here when Berri comes?

PROUT. Can't you say she's your wife?

PARTRIDGE. Of course I can't! My wife'll be here as well! She's only gone to the Embassy for brandy!

PROUT. I thought she was on sherry.

PARTRIDGE. The girl's certainly *acting* like a wife – nagging and moaning and throwing punches ... That's it! We'll say she's *your* wife!

PROUT. Well, if that's ... what?

PARTRIDGE. We'll tell Monsieur Berri Astrid is your wife. He'll be impressed – she's a good-looking woman. Could help your career.

PROUT. But I'm not married!

PARTRIDGE. Exactly. NATO worry about unmarried diplomats in their thirties. Black-mail risk, you know the sort of thing.

PROUT. I'm sorry, it's out of the question.

PARTRIDGE. So you'll let all this come out? Your bungling the lease of the flat ... your link with a shady businessman ... your covert homosexuality?

PROUT. Well no ... I mean, look ... even if I co-operate, will *she* co-operate?

PARTRIDGE. Co-operate?

PROUT. It's no use telling Berri she's my wife if she says she isn't.

PARTRIDGE. Nonsense. We just have to prepare him.

PROUT. Prepare him?

PARTRIDGE. Tell him she's your wife, but she likes to deny it. Bit potty ... tricky age, you know.

PROUT. You think that would work?

PARTRIDGE. 'Course it will – they're used to loonies in the Common Market. Tell him to ignore anything she says.

PROUT. Well. if Kibble can shift Mrs. Muller, we might just get away with it.

PARTRIDGE. Except for these blasted clothes. You told your girl the suits were urgent?

PROUT. Absolutely. *(The doorbell rings.)* That'll be her now.

(PARTRIDGE has been pacing about since ASTRID's exit. As he's nearest the front door, he goes to the hall to open it. We hear the front door open, and the voice of LADY PARTRIDGE.)

PARTRIDGE. Oh! ... it's you, my dear.

GILLIAN. I got back as quick as I could. How is the poor man?

PARTRIDGE. What poor man?

GILLIAN. The poor man who needed this brandy.

PARTRIDGE. Ah ... er ... nasty business ... terrible state ... I'm very worried ... *(PARTRIDGE and his wife now enter the lounge, LADY PARTRIDGE carrying a bottle of brandy and a small first aid box. PROUT has forgotten to lie down again, and is discovered sitting upright and alert.)* ... that's to say, he's a great deal better ... almost recovered ... well done, Prout ... I was telling my wife you've almost recovered.

PROUT. Ah yes ... I'm very much better. Thank you for getting the brandy, Lady Partridge.

(PROUT reaches out a hand for the bottle, but LADY PARTRIDGE holds it away and gives him the first aid box instead.)

GILLIAN. Oh good. As you're all right, perhaps I *could* take a little brandy after the sherry – they both come from grapes, don't they. I'm rather exhausted.

PARTRIDGE. Of course, my dear. Why don't you have a lie-down?

GILLIAN. D'you know, I think I might. What time's this big-wig coming?

PARTRIDGE. Quite soon – but you could have a little nap in the bedroom and then make an entrance.

GILLIAN. You will excuse me, Mr. Pratt ...

(LADY PARTRIDGE, still clutching the bottle, is making for the room LOUISE entered. PARTRIDGE moves swiftly across and opens the door of the other bedroom.)

PARTRIDGE. Use *this* bedroom, Gillian, it's much the more restful.

GILLIAN. I don't find this a restful flat. That reminds me, Mr. Pratt said we were going to the Mediterranean Hotel.

PARTRIDGE. Going to the Mediterranean?

GILLIAN. I've packed my bag all ready to move. When are we off?

PROUT. Er ... ah ... we had trouble with the arrangements, Lady Partridge. My staff are still working on it, but I'm afraid you may have to stay here.

GILLIAN. Pity. I get bad vibrations here.

PROUT. That'll be the boiler. We're trying to get it fixed.

PARTRIDGE. Come along, my dear, you have a good lie-down. Monsieur Berri would like to see you at your best! *(LADY PARTRIDGE enters the bedroom, and PARTRIDGE shuts the door behind her.)* Shame he's twenty years too late. What was all that about, Prout?

PROUT. I originally thought your wife was Mrs. Muller. I was trying to persuade her to go to the South of France.

PARTRIDGE. Pity you didn't succeed. Still, she's out of the way for a bit. How soon can you shift the other one?

PROUT. As soon as Kibble arrives from the Embassy. He'll have to be the one to tell her, as she thinks I'm a plumber. *(The doorbell rings and PROUT hurries to the hall to answer it.)* That may be him now. Or it could be Miss Jellicoe with our clothes.

PARTRIDGE. *(To himself, in the lounge.)* Or, the way things are going, it could be ten Bulgarian acrobats, with a troupe of performing seals.

(The front door opens, off, and the voices of PROUT and KIBBLE are heard.)

KIBBLE. I got back as soon as I could, Mr. Prout.

PROUT. All right, Kibble, hurry up – have you got Mrs. Muller's ticket?

KIBBLE, Yes, I have it here.

(PROUT now hurries KIBBLE into the lounge.)

PROUT. Mr. Kibble's got Mrs. Muller's ticket, Sir Clive. It's all right, Kibble. Sir Clive know about Mrs. Muller. He's being very understanding – as long as she's out of here before Monsieur Berri arrives.

KIBBLE. I've an Embassy car outside, Sir Clive, waiting to take her to the airport. There's a plane to the South of France in ninety minutes.

PARTRIDGE. Where is Monsieur Berri?

KIBBLE. I left him with the German trade delegation. He may be some time – he's trying to sell them French sauerkraut. And they're insisting the French buy German snails.

PARTRIDGE. Thank God for that.

KIBBLE. Is Mrs. Muller ready to leave?

PROUT. Er ... well, not quite, to be perfectly honest. We're rather depending on *you* there, Kibble.

KIBBLE. On *me*, Mr. Prout?

PROUT. Yes. There's been a slight mishap. The lady I was persuading to move turned out not to be Mrs. Muller at all.

KIBBLE. So Mrs. Muller isn't here?

PROUT. Oh yes, she's here, she's resting in the bedroom. But she doesn't know anything about moving.

KIBBLE. Then why don't you tell her, Mr. Prout?

PROUT. Er ... how shall I put it? ... well ... the thing is, you see ... *(He decides to take the plunge.)* ... Mrs. Muller wouldn't believe I'm a diplomat because I surprised her in the bathroom ... and also she caught Sir Clive and me on the settee, and we let her think we were on the job. And then there was the banging in the kitchen, and now she thinks we're plumbers.

KIBBLE. I'm not sure I follow, Mr. Prout.

PARTRIDGE. Good grief, man, never mind that! Just see Mrs. Muller and tell her she's to join her husband in the Mediterranean.

KIBBLE. Would she take any notice of me? No-one else ever does.

PROUT. That's because you don't assert yourself. Now's your chance to be a diplomat, Kibble. It's not too late. We may be looking for a new fourth secretary next year.

KIBBLE. Oh. Well, I'll see what I can do, Mr. Prout. Mrs. Muller's in the bedroom, you say?

PROUT. That's right. She's having a rest.

(The boiler starts a low ten-second rumble.)

PARTRIDGE. As she thinks we're plumbers, we'd better get into the kitchen, Prout. Don't want awkward questions.

PROUT. Quite right, Sir Clive, and the sooner the better. Good luck, Kibble – don't let us down.

KIBBLE. I'll certainly try, Mr. Prout.

PARTRIDGE. For God's sake, be quick, man! Tell her you're late and it's urgent!

(PARTRIDGE and PROUT hurry into the kitchen, and shut the door behind them.)

KIBBLE. Now then ... bedroom ... bedroom ... over here, I think ... *(KIBBLE goes to a bedroom door and knocks, unfortunately choosing LADY PARTRIDGE's room instead of LOUISE MULLER's. As he waits, he rehearses to himself.)* Excuse me, madame, I've come from the Embassy. I'm awfully late and it's urgent ... *(He tries a slight variation.)* Excuse me, madame, I've come from the Embassy. I'm late and it's awfully urgent ... *(LADY PARTRIDGE opens the door and peers out.)* Excuse me, madame ...

GILLIAN. My God, who are *you?*

KIBBLE. I'm from the Embassy. I've an awful urge, and it's latent.

GILLIAN. What!?

KIBBLE. I've an urgent message from your husband, there's been a change of plan. He wants you to join him in the Mediterranean.

GILLIAN. He changes his mind very quickly. *(She's somewhat bemused.)* Or have I been asleep? Where *is* my husband?

KIBBLE. He's there already – he flew off in a hurry. He's waiting for you.

GILLIAN. Oh well, I'll be glad to leave this place. The wall-paper in there seems hostile.

KIBBLE. You'll be happier in the Mediterranean.

GILLIAN. I know, I spent my honeymoon there.

KIBBLE. I've a car waiting outside.

GILLIAN. Well, my bag's still packed from earlier.

KIBBLE. May I carry it for you?

GILLIAN. Thank you.

(They enter the bedroom briefly, and quickly emerge, KIBBLE carrying the travel-bag LADY PARTRIDGE arrived with.)

KIBBLE. Is this all your luggage?
GILLIAN. Oh no! I've forgotten something vital ...

(LADY PARTRIDGE returns to the bedroom and comes out with the bottle of brandy, now half-empty. She closes the bedroom door behind her, and she and KIBBLE cross the stage to the hall. We hear the front door open, and then KIBBLE has a last-minute thought.)

KIBBLE. Ah ... er ... excuse me ... I have to check the gas is off in the kitchen ... *(KIBBLE hurries back, crosses the lounge, opens the kitchen door, and announces the good news in quiet triumph.)* I've done it, sir, the lady and I are leaving now! *(KIBBLE closes the door, then has an afterthought and opens it again.)* You won't forget, when that job comes up next year? *(Now KIBBLE hurries back to the hall, and we hear him pick up the case.)* Right, madame, we're all set ... after you ...

(We hear them leave and the front door close. PROUT and PARTRIDGE emerge from the kitchen in slightly happier mood.)

PROUT. One down and one to go!
PARTRIDGE. Thank God for that! Now how do we stand? My wife's resting in the bedroom ... Astrid's changing in the bathroom – but that's all right, we're passing her off as your wife ...
PROUT. Look, I've been thinking about that ...
PARTRIDGE. Well don't, it's settled. Now it's just these clothes. What's happened to your blasted secretary? Why isn't she here with the suits?
PROUT. I'm sure she's doing her best, Sir Clive. I've no doubt she'll be here any minute. *(The phone rings and PROUT picks up the receiver quickly.)* Hello? ... Miss Jellicoe!? Good grief, you should be *here*, not ringing up! Where are the suits ... Any minute? ... Where are

you ringing from? ... The office, and you're just leaving? Why did you take the clothes to the office? ... You haven't *got* the clothes? ... You haven't been to my flat yet, but you're just going now!? ... You've been in the office all this time!? But *why?* ... You had to finish the filing!? ... No. It's all right, Miss Jellicoe, don't bother now. I just hope you're happy at our Embassy in Tibet. *(Bitterly, PROUT replaces the telephone receiver.)* We're not getting the suits. Miss Jellicoe never left the office.

PARTRIDGE. My God, you've really screwed this up, Prout. Berri *must* be here soon – he has to leave at eight for a dinner. He'll arrive to liaise with his favoured successor, and find me looking like an elongated radish!

PROUT. Perhaps we should put the tunics on.

PARTRIDGE. Tunics?

PROUT. Yeoman's tunics – we left them in the parcel. Part of the costume.

PARTRIDGE. Costume?

PROUT. The Yeomen of the Guard costume. We'll look better wearing the whole thing.

PARTRIDGE. I can't receive Monsieur Berri wearing theatrical costume.

PROUT. I'm sure it's our best option in the time available. He'll think it's some sort of British ceremonial outfit. I'll show you.

(PROUT hurries into the kitchen, leaving the bewildered PARTRIDGE to sink slowly down onto the sofa, where he sits with his head in his hands, complaining sadly to the empty air.)

PARTRIDGE. Why does this happen to *me?* I've always led a decent life. Well, *fairly* decent. *Almost* always. I go to church at Christmas. I never fiddle my expenses, by more than twenty per cent. I've helped lame dogs over stiles ... even when they didn't want to go. And now *this* ghastly thing ... *(PROUT comes out of the kitchen, now in full beefeater costume, with tunic.)* Talking of ghastly things ...

PROUT. You see, Sir Clive, now I'm complete!

PARTRIDGE. Yes, a complete idiot!

PROUT. It's better than just the vest.

PARTRIDGE. Perhaps it is, but I won't wear it.

PROUT. If we say nothing, he'll suppose it's some sort of formal wear.

PARTRIDGE. I won't, I won't, I won't! *(The front door bell rings: a pompous ring, slightly longer than usual: followed, after a fractional pause, by another.)* My God, I'll have to!

PROUT. You think that's Berri?

PARTRIDGE. It *is* Berri – I recognize the ring.

(PARTRIDGE hurriedly disappears into the kitchen. PROUT sleeks backs his hair with his hand and crosses to the hall. We hear the front door open, and the voices of PROUT and BERRI.)

PROUT. Ah, Monsieur Berri, good evening. Please come in.

BERRI. Sir Clive Partridge is at home?

PROUT. Indeed yes, we were expecting you. I'm Simon Prout, British Embassy. *(PROUT and BERRI enter the lounge. BERRI is in his fifties, an impressive Gallic figure, somewhat stern and formidable. He wears an expensive overcoat, and looks askance at PROUT's strange attire.)* May I take your overcoat, Monsieur Berri?

BERRI. No, I cannot stay long. There was delay at the German Trade Mission. I was held up by the attachés.

PROUT. Oh dear. May I pour you a drink, sir?

BERRI. Certainly not, I never touch liquor. Alcohol is the scourge of Western Europe. It is hard to imagine a greater menace.

PROUT. You've met Sir Clive Partridge?

BERRI. Indeed. I have encountered him several times in committee. He seems to share my view of European needs. Morality, not munitions! Duty, not decadence!

PROUT. Er ... quite. He certainly takes his work very seriously. A great example to us all. A very upright man.

(SIR CLIVE now enters from the kitchen, in full beefeater outfit: his embarrassment causing him to stoop somewhat. He crosses to BERRI in rather hunted fashion, and offers his hand.)

PARTRIDGE. Monsieur le Président, good to see you again.

(BERRI is clearly astonished at PARTRIDGE's clothes, but shakes the proferred hand somewhat guardedly.)

BERRI. Good evening, Sir Clive. I thought we should have a brief talk before tomorrow's conference.

PARTRIDGE. Ah yes, the election, of course. Rest assured, Monsieur Berri, I'm your man.

BERRI. The election, yes. But first there are more pressing matters. The Milk Mountain, for instance.

PARTRIDGE. Ah ... indeed. Won't you sit down? *(BERRI and PARTRIDGE sit.)* I'm pleased to say, Monsieur Berri, that I've solved the Milk Mountain. All our surplus milk is on its way to Russia in refrigerated lorries.

BERRI. Not so, unfortunately.

PARTRIDGE. There'll be no more ... pardon?

BERRI. I have heard from the Euro-Milk Board. The milk started moving three days ago.

PARTRIDGE. That's right.

BERRI. The lorries were not properly refrigerated.

PARTRIDGE. Not properly refrigerated?

BERRI. Today we have a cheese mountain.

PARTRIDGE. But ... but ... it was all arranged. My staff ordered suitable transport last week.

BERRI. Unfortunately, they dealt through a shady operator, a confidence trickster, a man called Max Muller. He leased inferior vehicles and made off with the money to the South of France.

PARTRIDGE. My God!

BERRI. Sir Clive, strong language will not help. Careful planning is what the European Commerce Commission needs.

PARTRIDGE. Of course, yes, of course. But everyone makes mistakes.

BERRI. When you take over from me as President, you will find one cannot afford mistakes. There are many headaches.

PARTRIDGE. Ah yes, when I take over ... I take it I still have your endorsement, Monsieur?

BERRI. To tell you the truth, I have a headache now. Could you get me a glass of water, please?

PARTRIDGE. Of course ... at once ...

PROUT. I'll get it, Sir Clive.

PARTRIDGE. It's all right, Prout, I'll go. We're very democratic here, Monsieur Berri.

(PARTRIDGE hurries off to the kitchen, and PROUT – who has been hovering in the background while the senior men talked – picks up the tablet bottle which LADY PARTRIDGE brought out of the bedroom.)

PROUT. We have some pain-killing tablets, Monsieur Berri. Stronger than aspirin, I'm told.

BERRI. Very well. I do not object to drugs for medicinal purposes.

(BERRI takes the tablet bottle from PROUT and, with effort, removes the cap.)

PROUT. Two of those should sort you out, sir.

BERRI. I will take three, to do a proper job.

(BERRI pours three tablets into his hand and keeps them there, while replacing the cap and putting the bottle down. PARTRIDGE returns from the kitchen with a glass of water and hands it to him.)

PARTRIDGE. Would you like some ice?

BERRI. Thank you, no – I only need a sip.

(BERRI pops the tablets in his mouth and drinks some water to wash them down.)

PARTRIDGE. You may be sure, Monsieur, that when I become President on your recommendation, I ... *(PARTRIDGE stops in horror, realizing that the tablets BERRI has swallowed may come from the bottle at his side – the pills with which ASTRID threatened to kill herself.)* My God, what have you swallowed?

BERRI. Your colleague gave me these pain-killing tablets. You seem upset – could you not spare them?

PARTRIDGE. Yes ... no ... the thing is, they're pois ... poise ... possibly a little stale. Look, I'd like to discuss tomorrow's election. It *is* still your intention to recommend me?

BERRI. At this moment, I favour you against the other candidates, yes. It is a poor field.

PARTRIDGE. You're very kind. I wonder, could I have your endorsement in writing? In case you're unable to attend for any reason.

BERRI. Unable to attend? Of course I shall attend. This, for me, will be the finish!

PARTRIDGE. Yes ... I mean, perhaps a note to be on the safe side ... in case you're detained and someone else chairs the meeting.

BERRI. Someone else? As you British say, "over my dead body"!

PARTRIDGE. Well, it is a possibility ... you're ... er ... feeling quite well, Monsieur?

BERRI. A little dizzy, it is the headache. Listen, Sir Clive, I will recommend you tomorrow. You are not the most clever candidate. Nor the most imposing. I shall recommend you because you, like me, will set high moral standards ... the purity of soul, the respectability, the unyielding virtue which will restore the rectitude and dignity of Europe!

(The bathroom door opens and ASTRID comes out in bra and briefs and a bad mood. She is carrying her bedraggled dress, and she marches up to PARTRIDGE and thrusts it at him.)

ASTRID. You see, Poochy! You see what you have done! You make me have it off in the bathroom! And, look, my dress is ruined! I cannot clean it! I must borrow from your wife. I do not care if she know of our affaire!

BERRI. Mon dieu! Who is this? Do you know this woman?

PARTRIDGE. Er ... Prout ... this is your wife, isn't it? Your wife, Prout!

(PROUT moves reluctantly forward and swallows hard.)

PROUT. Er ... yes ... that's right ... Monsieur Berri, this is my wife!

BERRI. Then why does she call Sir Clive "Poochy"?

PROUT. Er ... it's a special British title, given to Heads of Department. Er ... come along, dear, put some clothes on, and we'll leave.

(ASTRID is astonished to see PROUT on his feet, having been told he was dying.)

ASTRID. You? What do you mean, your wife? What do you play at – you should be dead!

PARTRIDGE. *(Prompting PROUT.)* She's a little disturbed, isn't she ... tell Monsieur Berri how disturbed she is.

PROUT. Monsieur Berri, my wife's a little disturbed ... well, very disturbed ... an accident with a boiler ... I'm sure you understand.

(BERRI has progressed visibly from astonishment to rage.)

BERRI. No, I do not understand ... I do not understand at all!

PROUT. She's, well ... you know, a bit bananas ... un morceau bananes ...

ASTRID. You! You were not hurt at all, you tricked me! Now ... *now* you will be hurt ...

(ASTRID picks up BERRI's glass of water and hurls the contents at PROUT. It is almost a replica of her previous assault, as PROUT ducks and the water hits BERRI in the face.)

PARTRIDGE. Good grief, she's finally snapped! I'm so sorry, Monsieur Berri. Prout was trying to nurse her along, but she'll have to be locked up!

(PARTRIDGE grabs the dress ASTRID is carrying, and uses it to mop the water off BERRI's overcoat: PROUT assists with a handy table-runner. BERRI's anger has changed to bewilderment.)

BERRI. Alors! So she is mad! And you have been trying to help her?

PARTRIDGE. Absolutely! Purity alone is not enough, Monsieur. One must also have compassion.

(The phone rings. With PROUT and PARTRIDGE busy mopping BERRI's coat, it is BERRI himself who lifts the receiver.)

BERRI. That may be my office, they know I am here ... 'Allo ... what? ... Miss Jell ... what? ... Miss Jellicoe. A message for Mr. Prout ... and Sir Clive? What? ... Mon dieu! Yes, yes, I will tell them. *(BERRI's controlled fury has returned. He replaces the receiver, and addresses PARTRIDGE and PROUT in bitter tones.)* A message from your friend Miss Jellicoe – 'She is at your flat and willing to remove your clothes.' And her own, no doubt!

PROUT. No! No! I only asked her to get our trousers down!

BERRI. C'est incroyable! You have an undressed woman here, and a lady of the night at home! You are lechers, both of you! It is true about you British. There is so much vice in London, you export it to the Common Market! No wonder your Embassy has a Vice-Consul!

PARTRIDGE. No, no, it's all a misunderstanding ... isn't it, Prout!

PROUT. Absolutely. There's no vice at the British Embassy. All our staff are above reproach!

(Suddenly we hear raised voices in the hall. A furious LADY PARTRIDGE has stormed in, the front door having been left open on BERRI's arrival. She is accompanied by a bewildered and wounded KIBBLE, who is trying to placate her. The row quickly crosses the hall, and LADY PARTRIDGE storms into the lounge, with KIBBLE in tow. He is soothing his aching jaw with his hand. LADY PARTRIDGE is clutching her travel-bag.)

GILLIAN. Get away from me, you ravening beast! How dare you! I intend to call the police! ... Ah Clive, thank God you're here! I've been assaulted! Hi-jacked! This monster tried to rape me!

PARTRIDGE. Gillian! What on earth's going on?

PROUT. Kibble! What's happened?

PARTRIDGE. Exactly! What have you been up to, Kibble?

GILLIAN. Clive! You *know* this brutal sex-maniac?

PARTRIDGE. Not at all! ... no! ... well, that's to say, I've *met* him ...

PROUT. Mr. Kibble is one of our Embassy staff, Lady Partridge.

BERRI. So! All your staff are above reproach? It is as I thought! A cesspit of iniquity!

PARTRIDGE. Just a minute! Kibble, explain yourself!

KIBBLE. Well ...

GILLIAN. And now perhaps you'll hear my side! This fiend lured me to a car, saying I was to join you at the Mediterranean Hotel! But we drove past the hotel and out towards the airport! When I protested, he said he was taking me to the South of France – obviously for white-slavery!

BERRI. Mon dieu, you poor woman! What did you do?

GILLIAN. I got out of the car at the traffic-lights. He tried to restrain me, and I felled him with a karate chop. Lucky I took those evening classes!

KIBBLE. I didn't know this lady was your wife, Sir Clive. I thought she was your *other* woman.

BERRI. Sacré bleu! *Another* woman! And you have the audacity to seek high office in the Common Market? Even to be elected Chief Poochy! How many women do you have, you Casanova?

ASTRID. Too many! For months he has been deceiving me! He would be a sex maniac, if he had the strength!

PARTRIDGE. Ignore her, Monsieur Berri – she's mad, as we told you. Look, this decrepit old lecher assaulted my wife. Very well, he'll be expelled from the Foreign Service!

KIBBLE. But Sir Clive ...

PARTRIDGE. Be quiet! You tried to seduce Lady Partridge! You can't stay on with that lack of judgment! *(To BERRI.)* But the sins of this old goat don't reflect on the rest of us!

KIBBLE. Old goat?

PARTRIDGE. Don't keep butting in! The point is, Monsieur le Président, I am blameless. This lady is my wife. And that lady is the wife of Mr. Prout, alas somewhat unbalanced after years of association with the Foreign Office. And there you have it. There are no other women in my life!

(BERRI is bewildered.)

BERRI. You are very convincing, Sir Clive. One would like to believe you.

ASTRID. Believe him? Better to believe in Santa Claus! *(She confronts PARTRIDGE.)* Who was the woman in the bathroom?

PARTRIDGE. Woman in the bathroom? Prout, we must spare Monsieur Berri further embarrassment. Get your wife out of here at once!

GILLIAN. Just a minute, Clive, *I've* been wondering that. Who was that girl who appeared in a cloud of steam? Mr. Prout, you saw the girl, didn't you?

PROUT. Er ... did I? Well yes, it did look like a girl, I must admit. But one couldn't be sure, with all that steam.

GILLIAN. *(To PARTRIDGE.)* You seemed to know who she was, but you didn't want to say.

BERRI. A third girl here? Who would that be, Sir Clive?

PARTRIDGE. There isn't any third girl! There's no-one in the bathroom! See for yourself! *(PARTRIDGE strides across and throws open the bathroom door. As he does so, the door of the adjacent bedroom opens, and the unseen LOUISE addresses him from within.)* I tell you, there is no other woman!

LOUISE. Hey, Lover, why don't you quit yakking and get back on the job?

(PARTRIDGE is aghast. BERRI has now seen and heard enough.)

BERRI. So! One would have liked to believe you, Sir Clive, but one cannot. It is clear that you are a philanderer, a womanizer – quite unfit to hold office in the Common Market! I withdraw my approval – I shall urge the Conference to vote for another, more moral, candidate!

(PARTRIDGE, PROUT, GILLIAN, ASTRID and KIBBLE speak the following lines simultaneously.)

PARTRIDGE. But you don't understand, Monsieur Berri ...
PROUT. I'm sorry, Sir Clive, I did my best ...
GILLIAN. Now then, Clive, you'd better tell me everything ...
ASTRID. You see, it was true, what I said ...
KIBBLE. I don't think you've any right to call me a goat ...

(The babble of voices stops, as LOUISE emerges from the bedroom in a glamorous and revealing negligee. She is amazed at the throng in her lounge: but after a moment her eyes focus on Monsieur Berri.)

LOUISE. Who the hell are all you people, and why are you in my flat? And why aren't you goddam plumbers getting on with ... Frou-Frou! Lover, what are *you* doing here?

(She rushes to BERRI and throws her arms around his neck. All present react with astonishment, and BERRI with acute embarrassment.)

BERRI. Er ... I do not understand ...

LOUISE. How did you track me down, you clever old sexpot? You said we should only meet at our love-nest! How did you get my address?

BERRI. There is some mistake ...

LOUISE. Well, it doesn't matter now, Max has quit! I got champagne, we can have a celebration! You goddam plumbers get outta here, and take your floozies with you! Specially this broad in her next week's washing!

ASTRID. A broad? A broad? What is a broad?

LOUISE. Abroad is hell, baby. Abroad is full of foreigners, all acting crazy. Now will you people get outta here? *(To BERRI.)* Jacques, lover, it's been a long time, tonight we're gonna swing!

BERRI. No, no, I have a headache!

LOUISE. *(Giggling)* That's what you told me your wife always says! We'll soon straighten you out ... I'll go and put that champagne on ice ...

(LOUISE exits to the kitchen. All present are still dumb-founded. PARTRIDGE is the first to find his voice.)

PARTRIDGE. Well, well, so much for the puritanical Monsieur Berri. Monsieur Jacques Berri, who will lead Europe to new moral standards!

BERRI. Ah ... er ... I can explain ...

PARTRIDGE. No need, it's perfectly clear. Hard tack for everyone else, but lashings of crumpet for you. Pull up the ladder, Jacques, you're all right!

BERRI. Well ... we are all men of the world ...

PARTRIDGE. You won't be a man of this world much longer. Those tablets you took were poison.

BERRI. Poison? Mon dieu!

(BERRI collapses into a chair and slumps in a state of shock which could be mistaken for death. ASTRID picks up the tablet bottle which PARTRIDGE has indicated.)

ASTRID. Alors! So that is where my tablets went! I am glad I have found them – I take some now!

PARTRIDGE. Don't be a fool, Astrid! Killing yourself could ruin your life!

ASTRID. Idiot! These are not really poison – they are aspirins!

PARTRIDGE. Aspirins? You were bluffing?

ASTRID. You do not really think I'd kill myself for a man like you? I am glad I did not – I would not be alive to tell you I am leaving you. We are finished!

GILLIAN. I find this all very confusing, Clive. Why should Mrs. Prout kill herself? And who is that lady who's gone in the kitchen?

PARTRIDGE. She owns this flat, Gillian, Mr. Prout made a mistake in leasing it. However, all's well now. We'll move to the Mediterranean Hotel.

GILLIAN. Oh good, I'll find that much more restful. My bag is ready and waiting.

PARTRIDGE. *(Nodding toward the kitchen.)* And Monsieur Berri could say the same. If you have a spare dress in your bag, dear, perhaps you could lend it to Mrs. Prout, so she and her husband can leave. She had an accident with her own dress.

GILLIAN. I'll see what I can find. Come along, Mrs. Prout.

(LADY PARTRIDGE picks up her travel-bag and leads the sulking ASTRID into a bedroom.)

PROUT. When you say "All's well", Sir Clive, you may be forgetting tomorrow's election.

PARTRIDGE. I think not, Prout. I believe I shall have the whole-hearted support of Monsieur Berri now.

(BERRI, who has been sufficiently-conscious to take in the news of the tablets, now stirs.)

BERRI. Better, perhaps, if the tablets had been poison. My life ... my reputation ... they are ruined.

PARTRIDGE. Not necessarily. Those ladies didn't understand what was going on. And neither Mr. Prout nor I would reveal your guilty secret. Nor, I'm sure, will Mr. Kibble.

KIBBLE. It's very insulting to be called a goat.

PARTRIDGE. Just a joke, Mr. Kibble, I take it back.

PROUT. *(To KIBBLE.)* And I may well be putting up your name for promotion. This is a marvellous chance to show that discretion we talked about.

KIBBLE. *(Decisively)* I'm not the one to spread scandal, Mr. Prout, you know that.

PROUT. Good show, Kibble. And now perhaps you'd get back to the Embassy, and try and borrow suits for Sir Clive and myself.

KIBBLE. Very good, Mr. Prout. And I think I'll arrange some karate lessons.

(KIBBLE exits to the hall and front door: BERRI rises from his chair.)

BERRI. Sir Clive, I shall be pleased to recommend you to the Conference as my successor. We have more in common than I thought.

PARTRIDGE. Well, we're all human, Jacques. Even Prout here is almost human.

PROUT. We had a very accident-prone day, Monsieur Berri.

BERRI. Ah. Well, now we know each other better, may I perhaps ask you something which has worried me since I arrived?

PARTRIDGE. I can guess. It's our clothes, isn't it. You're wondering why we're wearing these costumes.

PROUT. It's easily explained, you see. Sir Clive lost it at the airport so Mr. Kibble was to look into his underwear but he dropped off the wrong whatsit and after I took off my clothes for Sir Clive somebody pinched my things. But we thought, as these were traditional British costumes, beggars can't be choosers and Bob's your uncle.

PARTRIDGE. Well, it's not quite as simple as that. But that *was* what you were going to ask?

BERRI. No. No, I wish to ask a favour. You see, after I left the German Trade Mission, I went briefly to the flat of a friend where I am staying – her husband being away, you understand.

PARTRIDGE. I understand.

BERRI. Unfortunately, their dog – a most ferocious animal – did not understand. Being extremely devoted to its master and entirely devoid of savoir-faire, the accursed creature attacked me, tearing my coat and trousers. It was a German dog, of course.

PROUT. Good Lord! What did you do?

BERRI. I had to improvise. Fortunately, my overcoat covers the result. But since I am here I have been too hot. I wish to ask – will you please not laugh if I take off my overcoat?

PARTRIDGE. My dear chap, as if we would.

PROUT. Allow me to help you, Monsieur Berri ...

BERRI. You see, all I had in my bag was my costume for the Belgian Embassy's production of The Desert Song.

(PROUT has now removed the overcoat, and BERRI is revealed in Foreign Legion costume.)

PARTRIDGE. My God, two Yeomen of the Guard and one Foreign Legionnaire! NATO's last line of defense!

(The release of tension and the comic spectacle presented by BERRI are too much for PARTRIDGE and PROUT, and they are pointing at the unfortunate Belgian and laughing at him as ...)

THE CURTAIN FALLS

PROPERTY LIST

Drinks cabinet, glasses and bottles
Key ring with two keys
Shredder (usually a small, safe-like cupboard in one of the
     walls)
Small bottle of tablets
Large brown-paper parcel with tight string containing two
     costumes for *Yeomen of the Guard* (or similar
     colourful production)
Tall shrub in a tub on the balcony
Small overnight bag
Small garden trowel
Small gardening fork
Tool bag containing a screwdriver
Two women's suitcases
Telephone
Two men's suits and shirts
Two or three small cosmetic jars
Colourful kimono
A bit of broken trellis (about 2 feet)
A toweling wrap
A long-handled bath brush
Bath mat with "Bienvenue" printed large on it
Light vase
Bottle of brandy
Small first aid box

OFFSTAGE SOUND EFFECTS

Hissing bath taps
A boiler rumbling and, finally, exploding